FATED GODDESS

ALSO, BY C. M. HANO

WORLD OF DALARIA

The Oath Of Blood And Roses

The Queen Of Ice And Stone

The Crown Of Ash And Shadow

RUTHLESS ROYALS

Fated Assassin

Fated Goddess

THE HUNTRESS SAGA

The Huntress

The Angel

WORLD OF CONSTELLINA

Once And Future Queen

Now And Forever Queen

Night & Day

Fated Goddess

Second Edition

Second Edition published 2026 by C. M. Hano LLC

Paperback ISBN: 979-8-9954671-7-5

Hardcover ISBN: 979-8-9954671-6-8

Cover design by: Elora Covers

Edited By: Ramona Mahi

Character Art: Brian Flores

Chapter Heading Designs: MSDesigns

To all the Queens that are slaying their demons one monster at a time.

1

FATE REVERSED

The damp smell of earth, echoes of war, and the cold stone beneath me pulled me from the last remnants of darkness. I blinked as the crystal lights flickered in the caves. My left palm pressed against my temple as I struggled to piece together what had happened. Every movement, every thought, was agony. Finally, I rolled onto my side, and that's when I saw him. Beaux. His chest wasn't moving. The perfect olive tone of his skin was pale, a stark reminder that he was dead.

"No!" I wailed, my throat scratching and burning with every painful emotion welling up inside of me. I crawled over to him, placing my ear against his chest, praying to Naxian to make it all go away. But then I already did that, so why didn't it work? I looked at my twin flame, brushing my hand over his cheek, the warmth of his skin replaced by ice. It sent a shudder through me, and guilt twisted in my stomach, making it hard to breathe. "I'm so sorry, Beaux."

This isn't your fault, Peech. Maya's voice rang in my head. I met her sympathetic gaze.

"I prayed to Naxian, begging for him to fix it all." Tears streamed down my face, my chest heaving with every sob that escaped me. I know, but it appears there has been another timeline manipulation. She responded, trying to provide me with some insight.

"He reversed it. I watched him snap his fingers and for a moment, like a dream, it felt as if I was Lasir herself," I admitted as distant memories flashed in my head. "Why would he take it back?" I asked angrily.

Maya was quiet for a few moments, her eyes closed shut as if she was searching for the answer in her head.

"Peech?" A soft voice broke through my grief, and I turned toward it. Relief washed over me as I saw my little sister, Patrice. Crawling over to her, she wrapped her arms around my waist as I brought her into my chest. "What happened? Why did that evil fae kill everyone?" I gently traced soothing circles down her back as she wept in my arms. When her sobs finally subsided, her tear-filled eyes met mine. In that moment, I knew I had to set my pain aside and be strong for her.

"Some fae are evil, Patrice. But you are safe and I will let nothing happen to you. After all, what are big sisters for if they can't keep their little sister safe?" I asked, and she nodded, a twinkle of a smile dancing in her eyes. I wiped her tears, and we held hands as we got to our feet. My eyes scanned the aftermath of the gruesome battle. Rue's decapitated head was a few feet away from her body, blood a pool around her. Tomas, the Fae king's body, was lifeless on the ground, with his cold eyes open and staring.

The feeling of his neck snapping between my hands filled me with pride. Then, I saw Demetri. He was slowly getting to his feet. I rushed over to him. "Your Grace."

He was off-balance momentarily as I pulled him into my embrace. "I'm sorry. I'm just relieved you're alive."

His eyes sparkled as he nodded, then backed away. “No harm done.”

Patrice hugged my guard, and I smiled, but then I caught sight of Beaux again. I walked over to Maya, touching my bonded dragon’s lowered head. “We need to bury him,” I said.

That isn’t the proper ritual, Peech. He was born a dragon-shifter and died a dragon’s death. The most appropriate and respectful ritual would be to send him to the Otherworld with dragon fire. She answered gracefully.

“So be it. Tell me what we need to do.” I commanded.

Gather as much wood as you can for a pyre. Then leave the rest to me. Demetri and I left the caves to gather wood, leaving Patrice with Maya. It eased my mind to know a dragon would be watching over her. The war began on the fields just outside of the Caves between Hazelberg. It was once a beautiful field covered in patches of snow, but now there is nothing but ash and blood—bodies of fae and humans scattered about.

Huddled just beyond the Firefang Forest, the border between the fae realm of Klanstia and Iticha, was a group of dragons. It appeared they were all looking down and talking to someone. I made my way over there, Demetri in tow, and through the enormous gaps, I saw her.

My Westend General Jen Josalen. Her sword was out, and I saw that fierce look in her eyes, then realized she probably thought the dragons were going to hurt her.

"Everyone, please move; you're scaring her," I said, and all eyes went to me.

The dragons cleared a path, and Jen raced towards me. We embraced like old friends.

"You're alive," she said in my ear.

"Yes. I'm glad to see you're unharmed, too. What is the current number of soldiers in the Iticha Armies? The cities?" I asked as we separated.

"Sierra, General Scarr is being held prisoner by a fae Warlord in Savannah. The fae armies have taken each city, including the capital," she responded grimly.

"Who sits upon my throne?" I asked.

Sierra visibly swallowed. "The Fae King has a daughter no one ever knew. Her name is Princess Plum."

“Never heard of her.” I tried to recall all the history I learned at Warrior Academy, but that name never came up. “Do we have any more details about her? Strengths? Weaknesses?”

Jen tapped a few buttons on her tele-watch, surprised it still worked after she’d transported us back. Moments later, a holographic video appeared, showing the princess marching up the steps to my palace. Her straight violet hair shimmered in the sunlight, and two onyx horns sprouted just above her pointed ears. When she turned, I expected her to resemble Mario more, but instead, she looked exactly like Beaux. Her bright violet eyes gleamed with victory, even from the tele-cam’s distance. Princess Plum wore a black leather jumper, knee-high laced boots, and a sword at her right hip. She gripped a large staff in her left hand, her sharpened claws clear, and her canines as sharp as her nails when she smiled. Then she said, “Point the tele-cam towards the people.” Fae soldiers lined the entire crowd with enormous weapons I’ve never seen before pointed at them.

“What are those?” I whisper-asked out loud.

“Where is the queen?” someone shouted.

The tele-cam shifted back to Plum's face as she raised an eyebrow and addressed the crowd. “Your queen has abandoned you. She left you here to pay for the consequences of her betrayal. But don’t worry. Princess Plum is here, and I’m going to ensure that peace and prosperity are my number one priority.”

“Our queen would never do that!” another person shouted and I felt a sliver of hope that at least some of my people haven’t lost faith in me.

“You, come here,” Princess Plum commanded. I swallowed hard as the tele-cam showed the man being pulled through the crowd by two faes. They brought him in front of the princess like a butcher brings a pig. She walked around him, scrutinizing his body. When she faced him again, she smiled before speaking. “You believe your traitorous queen to be loyal?”

“Yes,” he answered with pride. I expected to see fear, but there was none.

“Hmm. Then explain to me why she isn’t here?” Plum's gaze shifted to the crowd as she stepped forward, positioning herself so the man's back faced hers. “Why hasn’t your queen come to challenge me? I’ll tell you why, because she is a coward. My father,

Tomas Feynard, the Fae King of Klanstia, gave Queen Peech a chance at unity and peace. And you know what she did? Killed him and ran off with a bastard prince."

"She's lying," I said. "That isn't what happened, exactly."

"I know; she is trying to deceive them," Jen reassured me.

We kept watching as Plum strode back to the front center, her eyes gleaming with mischief. My heart began to thunder in my chest, bracing for whatever she was about to do next. A knot formed in my throat as I tried to speak, but it was already too late. "You will bow to me, your princess and ruler of both realms." Her eyes locked on the citizen in front of her. "Now. Bow."

He stood his ground, his posture firm. Then, without warning, her staff spun so quickly, slicing through air, flesh, and bone. He didn't have time to duck as his head tumbled down the palace steps, leaving a trail of blood behind. The crowd erupted into a mix of panic and rage. "This happens to those who will not bend the knee!" Plum's voice boomed across the city. "Submit or die. There is no other choice."

As the tele-cam zoomed in on the super princess's face, her eyes met mine, and in that moment, I knew she was challenging me.

Game on, bitch.

2

A NEW QUEST

The water from the caves cascaded around Beaux's body as I cleaned as much dirt, blood, and grim as I could. I would not let him go to the Otherworld like this. When he was clean, I wrapped him in the silk linens Maya got for me from Jen who scoured the decimated town for. With my new strength as the goddess of Fae and Flame, I could carry him to the funeral pyre we built just outside the caves. I laid him down, pressing a final kiss to his brow before I stepped back.

My body melts into his as he grips the back of my head, his hand tangles into my hair, forcing me closer to him. His tongue presses against my lips and I open to him, moaning at the taste of him—spiced cinnamon—my new favorite flavor. I feel him growing hard against me and I whimper at the size of him. That small surge I felt with every small contact of our skin turns electrifying, making my soul and body come alive. I need more. I want more. I want everything he offers me because at this moment, I feel nothing but complete.

He kisses me like a starving man seeing food for the first time. This isn't anything like the times Mario kissed me. It's all-consuming, earth shattering, and I know nothing will be the same after this. He once told me I was his forbidden fruit, but I think he was mine.

If you wish to give him a token so he may carry it on his journey to remember you, you must place it in his hands over his chest. Maya's voice snapped me out of my memory of our first kiss. I did as Maya instructed.

I looked at myself, but there was nothing but the rose silk dress I wore and my dragon bone dagger tight holsters, which my mother had gifted to me.

"What about this?" Patrice asked as she handed me a golden ring with a ruby shaped in a rose at the center.

"Where did you find this?" I asked her.

"Booth gave it to me just before that traitor Dasley captured us. He said I needed to give it to you because Mother wanted you to have it for your wedding day," she answered.

I inspected it, and then I remembered. "This was her mother's ring. I vaguely remember Queen Lasir wearing it. I was only four when she passed away from fever," I said.

"Did your grandmother get her name from the goddess?" Demetri asked.

"Yes," I whispered, looking at its beauty. Then I looked at my little sister and kissed her head before approaching the pyre. I grabbed Beaux's hands, slipped the ring on the tip of his right pinkie, and placed it over his heart. "In this life and the next, Beaux Kingston, I will find you again."

After the funeral, the ashes remained floating in the air, painting a gray contrast to the glowing moonlight. I watched every ember fade out until nothing but dust remained. Smoke cedar scent burning this memory into my soul when I looked towards Maya, the last of the flames flickered in her eyes, and I was grateful that she stayed by my side as Jen took over caring for Patrice, knowing I would need to mourn him on my own.

"Maya, how do I fix this? How do I save him? How do I save my people from this tragedy?" I asked, meeting her blue gaze, her white scales glistening in the moonlight. She was majestically beautiful.

"There are ways we can go about this, Peech. You can consult the caves as before or travel to Klanstia and seek a seer. Either will provide you with riddled futures. But the decision here is clear. Who will you save first? Your twin flame? Or the realms?"

There was a lot to unpack in those questions. I must ensure the realms are at peace again to give Patrice a safe future. How can I take it back without an army? It felt like a giant dragon seed was weighing heavily on my shoulders. Every decision carries a consequence, and the outcome depends on the choices we make.

I gazed at the stars, hoping they might offer some answer, but only a fool would seek guidance from balls of gas. My back pressed against the cool grass as I rested my head against Maya's side. Her warm body shielded me from the bitter chill of the Northend's eternal winter. She was asleep, the gentle sound of her snoring vibrating through her body. My eyes fluttered closed, the rhythmic movement lulling me into sleep.

"Why can't I come with you?" Patrice asked while I finished packing supplies for our trip across the border. Going to see a fae seer may not be the best plan, but I do not know what to do next. How do I take back my queendom without starting another war?

"Because it is not safe for you to travel with fugitives. Princess Plum has already sent a regiment of assassins and soldiers after us. I need you here where I know the dragon guild can protect you," I explained, touching her cheek softly. She doesn't budge or reply right away, so I kneel to meet her eye. "I love you, little sister. Everything that I do is to protect you. Please be good for Maya. Listen to her and stay safe."

Tears fell from her eyes, but she nodded, then wrapped her arms around me in a tight hug. "I love you, big sister. Come back home."

I gave her a brief kiss on her cheek before walking away, swallowing the lump of emotion swelling in my throat. Demetri and General Jen were waiting for me outside the caves. I gave them nods and looked up to Maya.

"Patrice will be safe. Princess Plum and her armies are no threat to me and my dragons," Maya reassured me.

A horse snorted to my far right, and I couldn't help but smile as I recognized the two steeds. "Barley? Bailey? Where did you two come from?"

Jen walked beside me as I ran my fingers through the thick manes. "While you were mourning, they crossed the border and waited. It's as if the gods above sent them to us."

"Barely is Beaux's horse. And Bailey is Barley's brother," I explained. "Let's get moving. The sooner we meet a seer, the sooner I can take my throne."

Jen and Demetri rode on Bailey together while I took Barley. I took one last long look over my shoulder, taking in the bright horizon painted across the decimated plains of Hazelberg. My heart thundered in my chest as I realized the color scheme—purple, gold, and pink. An artist dipped a brush into all three colors and stroked the skies. It was a sign from Beaux. A sign that there was hope that I would see him again and that the people of Itcha would be free again.

The last time I crossed this border was to broker peace with the King of Klanstia. Now, I'm crossing it to defeat his U-super daughter. Barley's hooves softly pressed into the brush of the Firefang Forest. There would be no need to push the horses at a slow pace at first, but then we kicked the steeds into a gallop. I went past branches and bramble, ignoring tree branches' scraps and near misses. Time was not on our side.

We stopped only to feed and water the horses, resting for a few hours to sleep. We doused the camp-fire before sunset to prevent it from attracting bandits.

"If I may ask," Jen started, "what made you break your vow to the Fae King?" I feared this question would come, but I was prepared to answer it. Jen leaned forward, and I knew she wouldn't judge me. As one of my most trusted generals, she deserved to know why so many of her soldiers had died. If she chose not to stand by me any longer, I wouldn't blame or punish her.

Because this was all my fault.

I looked at the stars as if they would aid me in my answer, but released a heavy sigh before speaking. "I met Beaux before we met with the Fae King. He was the one that helped scare Mario off. Not that I needed any help." Looking back on that moment, knowing the truth about Mario and Beaux's estranged relationship, I could see how much Beaux enjoyed insulting his half-brother. It wasn't just an opportunity to open the door between him and me, but a way to get back at his terrible half-brother without consequence from their demented father.

"He was the one you fought in the arena, wasn't he?" she asked.

I nodded my response. "I didn't know that, of course. But then, when we went to the peace dinner, and I excused myself from the table to get air, Beaux was there. Waiting for a chance to help us even when he was fighting his own battles, he was watching out for us." It was then I realized how meticulous everything he did was. The caution he took when we fought. The way he seemed to appear out of every shadow. Beaux was there to ensure I was safe. That if I needed the help, he would step in.

"You truly love him," Jen said, more than asked.

"There are not enough words to describe how I feel about him," I responded, and she gave me a small smile. It was not long after we settled I agreed to take the first watch. However, Jen and Demetri kept telling me I was a queen and needed to stand guard. I had to command them to get some sleep. How useful can two soldiers be if they get too exhausted to stand up?

The forest was quiet. It was the most peaceful time since the fighting began. Fireflies danced in the distance, a chorus of tiny insects that could lull every beast in the forest to sleep. My heart stung with the pain of remembering why we were here—and he wasn't. A few tears let go, biting my cold cheeks, and I let them fall. I was a warrior and a leader, and I couldn't let them see me like this.

'Let go, Your Grace,' Beaux's voice came from the shadows.

I looked around, praying to see him. Hoping that his death was a nightmare, and I feel his lips on mine waking me. 'Fight. No matter what. Fight. Fight. Fight.'

I snapped awake.

Blinking the brain fog from my eyes, I looked up to find Jen and Demetri immersed in conversation as they loaded the horses. It was only a dream. My heart squeezed in my chest, tears briming the rim of my eyelids as my fingers curled into fists. Of course it was, you got him killed. That small voice was back again, reminding me of my failures as queen.

I rose, dusted on the debris, and approached them. They turned to me, bowing with a morning greeting. "How long was I asleep?" I asked.

"About five hours," Jen responded. "Your Majesty."

"You don't need to do that," I said without thinking.

Jen and Demetri gave me a confused look. "I'm not the queen of anything right now. Just call me Peech. And no more bowing."

They both physically flinched as if I just stabbed them in the chest with my daggers. "May I speak freely?" Demetri asked, and I nodded. He looked at Jen for encouragement, which she silently gave him. "I remember the first time I laid eyes on you. We were right here in the forest. Our orders were to take you prisoners to negotiate with the Fae King for money.

There were five of us, and you challenged our leader to fight for your freedom. I didn't know it then, but I thought you were a fool. You proved us all wrong when you killed him. That took courage. I saw you stand up and fight your enemies. You didn't hesitate or use insults to delay in the middle of a battle. But you led the charge every time."

My heart was thundering at the admiration reflected in their eyes.

Jen spoke next, "We grew up together. We attended Warrior Academy together, and although this was the first war we had to fight in, you stood at the center of the battlefield. You've always known when you needed to take advice versus give it. A true leader is what our world has always needed. You maintained peace for so long because of your being. You are not our queen just because it's your birthright."

Jen and Demetri took a knee, withdrawing their swords in a pose of allegiance. "We pledge our life and sword to you, Queen Peech of Itcha. With all due respect, Your Majesty, we will not address you informally. You are the queen." My eyes stung with unshed tears as their trust and loyalty began to mend the shattered pieces of my soul. It would take more than just two loyal generals to heal me completely, but this was a start. “I feel honored to be your queen.”

3

A RISKY SITUATION

The Firefang Forest quickly reminded me of the origin of its name. Every thorn that snagged my clothes or pricked the exposed skin on my shoulders made me hiss in pain. The constant buzz of insects swarming around heightened my senses, leaving me on edge. One small sting from a firebug could cause a grown adult to break out in hives. Pustules that were painful with every small movement of muscle and the only cure was having a mixture of urine and salt pressed into the wounds.

As we drew closer to the murderous foliage, its thorns the darkest shade of blood, I couldn't help but think how getting cut by one would be like allowing a basilisk shifter's venom to drip onto your skin. A shudder ran through me at the memory of my experience with that venom.

"The Klanstia village is just beyond the bush line," Demetri said as he and Jen used their swords to cut a path.

"I was thinking the same thing," Jen said as she approached my side. "It's nearing noon. The streets should be filled with merchants and patrons seeking their lunch."

"We should go on foot from here, Your Majesty," Demetri suggested, and we all agreed. We were tying the Barley and Bailey to a nearby tree trunk.

I brushed Barley's main and whispered, "Stay put. But fight like hell if someone tries to steal you from us."

The horse's neigh was a good enough reply for me. Our footfalls echoed eerily throughout the misty morning air. Evidence of the brisk early morning meeting the heat from the approaching afternoon. Sweat formed on my brow as we scanned the area. Not a soul to see. We passed by closed doors to taverns, tailor shops, and bakeries, all with a posted sign noting they were not in operation.

"This isn't right," Demetri said, and I noted the leery tone in his voice.

My senses were on high alert the deeper we went into town. A beating of the drums caused us all to move. We formed a circle with our backs touching and weapons drawn, ready to defend each other to our last breaths. Only another drum sounded. Then another, almost as if it was leading an army into battle. Without speaking, we followed the beat and happened across a crowd. I gestured for them to sheath their weapons as I did, too.

There was no need to cause unwanted panic and bring attention to ourselves. If someone recognized me, a fight could break out. Or the fae soldiers would surround us, and I'm not comfortable using my new powers around innocents. If I tap into them and hurt someone else…my gut twisted at the thought of causing more pain and suffering.

Jen tapped on the shoulder of a young woman. A little girl was perched on her right hip. Their hair was matching and style. Auburn braids kissed the waistband of their plaid skirts. "Excuse me," Jen started. "What is going on?"

The woman looked at Jen with azure eyes. "How have you not heard about the execution?"

"Execution?" this time, I spoke, stepping closer. "Who?"

"The fae soldiers who failed to kill the traitor human queen." The woman's eyes looked accusingly at me. Jen and Demetri moved to form a wall between me and her. The drum beat stopped, and our attention turned to a raised platform ahead. The sound of marching boots and clattering chains reverberated through the town. An echoing in my ears that had my hands balling into fists at my sides.

I watched a masked man with broad shoulders wielding an ax come first. Behind him was a fae dressed in the same formal wear Tomas, the Fae King, wore. Medals, which the fae awarded their armies, decorated the crimson leather vest. A sword swung on his right hip, and I looked at his face, trying to figure out what kind of shifter he was. To no avail, but then I saw something glinting on his collar—a purple plum pin with a silver bar running across.

Was this an ambassador from Princess Plum?

When the drum beat stopped, someone answered my voiceless question and all I could hear was the rattling of chains. Linked were five faes. Three women and two men all stripped naked. Bruises, dirt, and dried blood covered their bodies. Signs of being wiped littered their backs, with some lashes still fresh. Bile rose in my throat despite the mistreatment and undeserving sentence of these soldiers.

My eyes fluttered back to the fae in charge as his voice rose out. "On this day, we bring justice to the realm of Klanstia. These five so-called generals betrayed your king, your princess, in the battle with Itcha by abetting the human queen."

The crowd insulted the prisoners, sitting at their feet and throwing rotten food and even some animal scat. I moved forward, but Jen and Demetri blocked my path.

"Now is not the time, Your Majesty. There are far too many of them," Jen warned.

She was right, of course, but it didn't lessen the rage burning inside of me. I couldn't just stand here, watching innocents get executed under false allegations of helping me. "Jen, we need to help them."

"We have no power here," she hissed back.

As the constable kept reading the charges and the executioner prepared to carry out the sentence, I scanned the area. My head recalling with different scenarios that would play out helping them. If I could use my powers without endangering civilians, then… Someone suddenly grips my wrist, interrupting my thoughts.

My attention snapped to the left, where Demetri subtly gestured toward the right side of the crowd. As my gaze swept over the area, noting its near-empty state, we moved in that direction, slipping through the outer edges of the crowd while keeping my head on a swivel. We reached the far left of the stage, where the staircase stood, and I looked at the chains binding the prisoners together. Closing my eyes, I focused on the links, pushing my power against them, but something was blocking it.

"What's wrong?" Jen must've noticed my struggle.

"There is something blocking my powers. I can't break the chain. It's like there is a shield around it," I whispered.

"Iron. They make the chains from iron. Look at their wrist." Demetri subtly pointed without gesturing, and my gaze shifted to the prisoners. I didn't waste any time thinking it over. Acting on instinct, I reacted without further hesitation. "Jen, get back to Patrice and keep her safe," I commanded, her eyes locking with mine in confusion. "I have to save them."

I turned on my heel, racing to the platform steps and jumped. Kicking my feet out, I heard the executioner's bones snap in his neck. His ax clattering to the floor. There was no time to wait as I drew my sword, connecting blades with the other guard that stepped between me and the constable. Sparks coming to life at the connection of our blades.

"Who is that?" someone shouted from the unruly crowd. But I ignore them, blocking another attempt at my head. I rolled forward, slicing at the soldier's ankles. He jumped at the last second, falling face-first on the ground at the crowd's feet. I took this moment of reprieve to place my blade at the constable's neck. Narrowing my eyes at him with as much authority I could muster up, I spoke, "You will release them. Or you will take their place." It was as if the goddess in me took over because there was no resistance. The keys rattled in his gloved hands as he went to the lock of each of them. The restraints dropping heavily to the wood platform. My gaze met the five fae. A mix of relief and fear in their eyes. "You are all free now. You may return home."

"But they're traitors," someone yelled.

"That is a lie," I responded, looking to the anxious mob. "Your princess has filled your ears with false truths. These fae did not aid me in the war. I do not know them, and I'm sure they do not know me."

"You're Queen Peech?" It was the little girl we saw earlier. Her minor figure was still clutched in her mother's arms at her hip.

"I am. Your king brought this war about. Tomas Feynard didn't want peace. He wanted to take over the entire realm." They were quiet, waiting for me to explain further. "I am at fault for this war. Your king and I would have to be married, but I ended the engagement. None the less, that doesn't mean there should be war between us. Humans and fae have lived in peace for decades. Yet, the hate between species continues to tear us apart."

"Didn't you run off with his bastard?" a man asked.

Beaux being referred to as a bastard. "It's a shame you think of your prince like that." I scanned the faces looking at me. Some wore hatred in their eyes, as if they'd relish seeing my head on a spike. Others looked on with curiosity. Those were the ones I needed to reach. “Beaux Kingston gave his life for the peace between us. He ensured I would live so that the realm could survive.” My voice choked as un-shed tears swelled in my eyes. “Beaux believed in peace so much that he did everything he could to fight the tyrant king. You should honor your fallen prince.”

“You killed him!” one of the fae accused. “He was your bodyguard, but you seduce him into your bed. Brainwashed him with your human ideals and now we don’t have our princes or king. But Princess Plum will make you and your followers pay. Kill the human queen!”

This was not good.

The mob rushed the platform, but something unexpected happened. The fae prisoners formed a circle around me. I could feel some of them using what little strength they had to form a magical shield around me. Soon, I was being pulled from the stage by Jen. Demetri and one of the male prisoners led us down an alley, through a house or two, until racing down a flight of stairs into some kind of bunker. Debris from above us started falling with the chorus of the mob's boots racing to catch us.

We paused a moment to catch our breath, and I looked at the male fae. His crimson eyes and dark black curls looked so familiar to me. He nearly reminded me of Beaux. I blink because that wasn't possible. I watched Beaux's body burn. His body perfectly laid out on the cedar pyre, he looked so peacefully asleep that if I just brushed a kiss to his lips he would wake. But that isn't what happened. I shook those painful thoughts away at the sound of the male fae's voice. "We should keep moving, Your Grace," the male fae said, and even those words sounded like Beaux.

"Who are you?" I asked him.

Everyone else looked at him and he scanned all our faces. "I'm going to be dead, as well as all of you, if we do not keep moving."

I shook my head at him, then closed the distance, my small dagger coming out in one swift movement to press against his neck as his back hit the wall. His arms came up into a surrender as a sly smirk came across his face and his eyes glistened with mischief. "Who are you?"

He didn't answer me right away. I looked deeply into his eyes, then did something I never thought of doing in all of my life. Leaning forward, I pressed my nose to the side of his neck and inhaled his scent. My eyes closed at the euphoria of it. Cinnamon, sandalwood, and dirt. Of course, he was dirty. But how could his scent be twin to Beaux's? That just wasn't possible, right? He'd been a prisoner for only gods know how long. To my surprise, he showed less fatigue compared to the others.

Memories of Beaux resurface, but I stepped away from the fae. "What kind of fae are you?" It seemed like my interrogation would not cause any answers. Footfalls raised alarm and snapped me out of my stupor long enough to know he was right. "We will finish this conversation later. But for now, if you would please lead us to safety, I would appreciate it."

"As you wish, Your Grace." He enunciated those last two words, each one smooth as wine rolling off his tongue.

"Queen Peech?" Jen grabbed my forearm, and I looked at her. "Is everything okay?"

"Yes." No. This fae was some kind of illusionist, and I did not trust him. "Let's go."

We moved along the underground hallway made from limestone and motor. I stayed behind Demetri and the male fae. Jen was at my back along with the other four fae. My dagger was in my right hand while my sword was in my left. Keeping my eyes on the path ahead, I was ready for any trap or betrayal this male fae could lead us to. It was then I realized oil torches instead of the crystals we use in Itcha illuminated the hallway.

The air is thick and moist. Sweat drips from my face. I wipe it onto my sleeve before it can get into my eyes. It seemed the deeper we went, the hotter it got. The hall grew narrower the further we went, pressing us closer together. A rancid smell emanated from the other fae, and I made a mental note that a place with a bath or a water source would be essential for them to clean up. Then my throat dried up, and my mouth ached to drink something. I soon found myself between Jen and Demetri.

"How much further?" one of the other fae males asked from the back.

"Not much," the male fae in the front answered. I really hope he's not leading us towards some hidden volcano. My nose smacked into the back of Demetri's head as we came to a sudden stop. The ripple affecting all of us as we braced ourselves on one another. My blades scrapping against the limestone walls.

"Once we go past this door, there is no turning back," the male fae explained, and I feel like everyone was waiting for my permission. I nodded.

A burst of cool air kissed my skin on the other side. We flowed into this new area like water does when a damn breaks. I looked around and noted there was a single log cabin on the other side of a large lake. An evergreen forest surrounded us on all sides. I've never seen this part of Itcha or read about a place matching this description in Klanstia lore books.

The male fae approached me, offering me a hand, but I didn't take it. "Where are we?"

"Come with me, and you will get all the answers you seek," he responded with a smile. I glanced past him at the cabin, then looked back over my shoulder. The door was gone, replaced by towering pine trees. I turned to face him again, and he said, "The only way forward is to never turn back. Remember what you're trying to accomplish, Your Grace. You need answers. I've brought you to the place that will give them to you."

Was he trying to tell me that a fae seer lived here? There was something telling me that other fae were here other than those currently in my presence. I didn't want to trust this man. Could it be that fate brought us this far?

"Your Majesty?" Jen asked as she stepped up next to me. I didn't need to show any doubt about myself. Not that I was worried about losing her support, but a good leader thinks with a level head. Decides based on what is right and instinct. 'Trust in yourself, Your Grace,' Beaux's voice reached out to me beyond the veil again, 'If the seer is in there, then we will decide about our next move.' I looked at the others, then let out a heavy sigh, holding my head high as I nodded. "Very well. Take me to the seer."

4

THE SEER'S PATH

The floorboards creaked with each step we took. Our weapons were returned to their sleeves once we sensed there was no danger lurking in the shadows. I watched as the male fae approached the door. It was normal sized, and nothing about the outside of this home told me a fae lived here. Jen and Demetri, self-proclaim bodyguards, stepped up to put space between me and whoever was owner of this house. Three knocks. No more. No less.

The door opened and a warm glow from candles welcomed us as we followed the male inside. Once we were all in, the door slammed shut, causing a shutter to run through my body and possibly the others. My hands instinctively went over the hilts of my weapons, but I relaxed when my gaze landed on an older fae sitting at a table with a crystal in the middle. He had cropped short silver hair above his pointed ears, the flicker from the dimly lit candles highlighted the crimson robes he was wearing, casting eerie shadows that accentuated his sharp, angular features. He folded his withered hands and placed them on the wood tabletop.

I cautiously approached him while examining the rest of the living area. There was nothing but a single rug and fireplace. A staircase led to upper levels, and another threshold connected to a kitchen from what I could see. I stepped to the edge of the table and then gestured to Jen and Demetri to go scope out the rest of this place.

"Aren't you going to ask permission before sending your dogs to invade the rest of my house?" the old fae asked. The question stopped the two in their paths.

"Forgive me. It would bring me great comfort knowing we were alone."

"But we aren't, Your Grace," he retorted. I thought about how to ask, but then he spoke again, "Your guards may look, but do not touch a single thing or else they will sleep outside." His cold grey eyes narrowed, as if his word was the law and we were meant to follow.

"Thank you," I responded, then nodded at the pair, waiting for orders. "May I sit?"

"How else am I going to read you?" he asked, and I took that as a sign to sit. Pulling out the chair next to him, I flinched at the fur ball curled on the blue cushion. "That is Bizzy. She won't bite…hard."

He hissed the cat away and gestured for me to take its place. The cushion was surprisingly comfortable. I adjust the loose tendrils sticking to my face. "You will fetch the queen some drink and a wet cloth."

I scanned the room to see who he was talking to but couldn't pinpoint anyone. The other fae that traveled with me were also sitting around the table. But in seconds, a drink of water appeared in my right hand, and a cool cloth pressed against my forehead. My reflection in the cup showed my eyes as wide as saucers. I must look like I've never seen magic used before in my life.

"Thank you," I stammered, bringing the cup to my lips. A moan nearly escaped me as the crisp, cool liquid coated the dryness of my throat. The cup was empty sooner than I wanted it to be. I set the cup down and locked eyes with the seer. His face was lined with wrinkles giving away his age. Freckles were in asymmetrical patterns across his nose and cheeks where silver eyes scrutinized me.

"Let me see your palms, Your Majesty," he asked. I offered them up. I expected cold calloused hands to brush against mine but his were smooth and warm. Like a newborn's. "I'd like everyone else to leave the room. There are separate bathrooms in each of the three rooms up top. Pick a bed and stay in there until I ring you for dinner."

Without protest, the five fae stood and did as they were told. This fae commanded respect. I admired him for it. Once the room cleared, I let out a calming breath and then refocused on the seer. "What is your name?"

"You know as well as I do fae names hold power." He raised a white brow, then smiled a toothless grin. "Close your eyes, Your Majesty. I believe you will finally get the answers you seek. After all, you are the Goddess of all Fae."

I swallowed hard but did as I was told. Darkness was all I saw at first. Then, the seer started to speak in the old fae language. Words started as foreign, but the images came to me as I focused on each syllable. "Fated goddess, clear your mind. Whatever you do, do not let go. No matter what you hear. The shadow fae will play tricks, so don't let them."

"Okay. I'm ready." I closed my eyes, focused on clearing my mind as images started to form in front of me. A field of wildflowers, the fresh scent of floral wafting over me like perfume. And the warmth from the sun kissed my skin. I looked around and saw a little girl dancing with butterflies just a few feet in front of me. Her auburn hair was braid tightly to the back of her head, the tail of it kissing her waist. It was eerily identical to mine. She turned around to face me. A smile came across her face as her eyes met mine. I wanted to go to her and pick her up.

But something was telling me not to move. To let this vision play out. The little girl closed the distance between us. The pink skirts of her dress blending in with the wildflowers dancing at her feet. She stopped just a foot in front of me and offered me the dandelion she has picked. I looked into her eyes, a stunning mix of crimson and blue. A color I'd never seen before. It wasn't quite violet but more like blue with red glitter sprinkled in.

"Will you take my gift, goddess?" she asked me. Her voice soft and reminding me of Patrice. My fingers itched to touch it, but instinct told me not to, the seer's warning playing on repeat in my head. The little girl stepped closer, the toes of my boots brushing against her bare feet. Her little fingers grabbed my hand before I could snatch it back and placed something in my palm. It wasn't the flower but smaller and round. I moved my hand up to examine the object. It was the ring that Tomas had given to me. The ring that was stolen and could enhance a faes power.

I looked to the little girl again only this time it was my fallen general, Dasley, at my feet. Her face was covered in dried blood and soot from a fire. "Dasley? How are you here?"

"I don't have time to explain myself. Take the ring and put it on. Forgive me, Your Majesty." Then she was gone. Just like that. In a matter of a second, I found out that Dasley was killed, but somehow, she had gotten the ring and gave it to me. I was starting to get a good idea of where I was. But the question of how a seer could send me here was put on a mental list to ask later. The ring was heavy and warm. It felt different from what I remembered, and I wasn't going to wear it. I placed it into the pocket of my pants.

The vision started to melt away. Wildflowers replaced with fire, the ground beneath my feet turning to obsidian. A cool air was replaced with heat from a volcano. I was standing inside of a literal volcano. Looking around to see if another person from my past was near by, I saw nothing and no one. My feet started moving on their own, and I walked closer to the edge. A river of lava waiting to devour me. I couldn't stop as I got closer and closer. I could feel blood rushing in my ears as my chest started to feel heavy and my heart thundered with panic.

"Help!" The scream echoed around the area. No one was in here.

"Do not let the shadow fae win!" the seer shouted.

My mind was racing with ideas. Hands feeling my body for weapons, but I guess they didn't travel with me here. Then I felt it in my pocket. The small little trinket that has caused so much pain and suffer-ing. As the lava started to pop, a sprinkle of it landed on the tip of my boot. Hot and sizzling, the leather started to melt.

"Fuck it." I quickly pushed the ring on my right hand and called on the power. I closed my eyes and fell. The anticipation of being burned alive was doused by strong arms wrapping around my waist and hailing me backwards. I impacted the ground hard and rolled jumping to my feet then getting into a fighting stance. But when I saw who it was, I nearly died from relief.

"Still trying to get yourself killed, Your Grace?" Beaux Kingston was standing in front of me. That sly smile playing across his gorgeous face. I examined him from head to toe and wing tip to wing tip. He was wearing the same outfit we had burned his body in.

"Beaux? Is it really you?" I asked. My heart hopeful as I stepped closer to him.

"In the flesh. Well, more or less," he answered, and I couldn't stop what happened next. I raced into his open arms, crushing his lips to mine. Beaux wrapped me in a tight embrace. He started kissing me back. Our tongues clashing together and I dug my fingers into his curls.

"How? Oh, gods. I missed you so much. I'm so sorry, Beaux." I was sobbing in his arms. My tears soaking through his shirt, but he rubbed a calming hand up and down my back.

"I'll explain everything, for now, kiss me," he said, and I didn't waste a moment longer. Our kiss was long and full of desire. Heat flooded my core and I could feel his erection pressing against me. Sensual thoughts came to life and my nails pulled his shirt up over his head. It fell to the floor. I saw the fresh scar still pink from the fatal wound he'd taken saving my life. I pressed a soft kiss to it. His muscled tightened under my touch and I moved lower. Committing ever part of him to memory.

"This is a dream, isn't it?" I asked before kneeling in front of him. Beaux followed my movements so we would be eye to eye. His warm hand gripped my face pulling my lips to his again. My face was wet from the tears that didn't seem to stop flowing.

"You gave me this." He pulled up the ring I had placed on his pinky only it was around his neck on a rose gold chain. "I don't know if this is a dream, but I do know that I have to tell you something."

"What?" I asked, listening intently.

"In order for you to bring peace to the realm, you have to marry a fae of royal blood. You have to accept the ring and the crown. It's the only way to defeat Princess Plum," he explained, and I nodded. Trying to understand and figure out how I could marry anyone other than Beaux.

"You and Mario are dead. And even if that bastard was alive, I'd kill him again before ever considering to be his wife." Beaux smiled at that.

He pressed his forehead to mine then inhaled my scent just as he always has. "I have to tell you something else. It's only that I found out recently when I came to the veil." Something loud caught my attention and I looked around again. We were still in the middle of a volcano only it felt like we had a shield around us. Beaux must have sensed my unease because he said, "We are protected." Beaux raised the ring again. "You sent me with a piece of you, the kiss you gave to me it adds a barrier of protection around me while I'm here."

In the moment I could feel the glimmer of magic surrounding us. The perfect bubble of peace, guarding us from the chaos erupting all around us.

"Okay. Please continue, although I can't imagine being anyone's wife other than yours," I admitted.

He smiled. "You're going to have to, Your Grace. To achieve our dream of continued peace."

"But who? I'm sorry, but your sister doesn't appeal to me either. Not that I wouldn't marry her. It's just psycho killer of innocence and usurper isn't something I want to marry."

He laughed. It was deep and rumble through me. A feeling I hadn't felt in a while came to life inside of me again. It was warm and tasted on those biscuits I always loved eating with Patrice. And then it hit me, I was happy. Even for a few minutes, I was happy again. "Hold onto that feeling when you leave here, Peech."

He said my name. "Say it again."

"I love you, Peech." I kissed him again.

"I don't want to marry anyone else. I need to be your wife. How can I bring you back? I'm supposed to be this all-powerful goddess, and I can't reincarnate you?"

Beaux shook his head. "Listen to me. You must find my cousin and give him this." He pulled the ring off his neck and clasped it around mine. It looked so small in his hand as he brought it to his lips.

Whispering inaudible words into the gem before I felt magic zap between us. It glossed a bright pink and he let it go.

"What did you do?" I asked. He was starting to fade in and out like a bad connection with a hologram. "Beaux Kingston, you cannot leave me again."

"Peech, you will give this to him. He will be the one you marry. You must do it before you face my sister or else there will never be peace."

"Beaux, what did you do?" I screamed, grabbing at his image, but my fingers went through it again.

"Find the crown. Perform the ceremony of unity. I love you." His image and voice faded into the darkness, and when I opened my eyes again, the seer had let go of me. Something bright pink caught my attention and I looked down to see the ring vibrating against my chest. The seer reached out to dab my cheeks with a cloth then gently gripped my chin.

"You're one of the strongest women I've ever met, Your Majesty," he spoke as if he had known me my entire life. "If you need further assistance, then I would be honored to help you."

I met his gaze—it was filled with admiration and respect. Reflecting the feelings I had for him.

"Thank you." I almost said his name allowed but kept it quiet. Then whispered, "Kristoff."

He blinked, then nodded. "Now that you know what must be done, will you do it?" I stood this time, walked over to the single window that looked out from the dining table we were at, then sighed. "Our realms were at peace, but the only way to guarantee it would be through a marriage proposal. Which Tomas and I agreed upon."

I paused to see if Kristoff would ad-lib, but he remained quiet. The sun was descending beyond the trees, and snow started to fall. "Did you know that I would see him?"

Kristoff came up to my side. "I suspected. But it was your journey to take. Everything that happened in there was real."

"Meaning?"

"Meaning that you would've died if you fell in the lava." Of course it was real. My fingers traced my lips that still lingered with Beaux's kiss. "He was real."

"And the little girl? Who was she?" I asked.

Kristoff didn't answer me right away because I knew who she was. I just didn't want it to be true. "You tell me."

There was no mistaking who she was. The moment I saw her eyes and felt her presence. She was familiar to me. “My daughter. But how is that possible when my twin flame is dead? I don’t know if I can bring myself to love another.”

Kristoff grabbed the glowing ring then held it to my face. “He told you to give this to the fae you are to marry. That is your answer, Your Majesty. If you want to end this war.”

I blinked away tears then released a breath. “Can you help me?”

“The man you seek is already here. As for the crown, you’ll have to go back to the Klanstia palace and retrieve it. It still lies with the late-king.”

“What does that mean? Tomas is dead.” Then I trailed off as Kristoff touched my temple pushing an image of a tomb with the crown inside of it resting on the dead body of Tomas Feynard. “Now I have to be a grave robber.”

“And you will marry him before you leave my realm,” he commanded. “Go to the hot springs behind my cabin and give yourself a good cleaning. I’ll have someone bring you some clean clothes. I assume you can conjure heat to keep the winter breeze from chilling your bones?"

"Thank you." I made my way towards the back of the log cabin through the hall that was under the stairs. When I crossed into the kitchen and opened the back door, I was instantly smacked in the face with snow. I saw the steam rising from the hot springs only twelve feet or so from the back porch. Making my way down the small set of stairs, I walk to the water's edge. I couldn't see past the mist to know I was alone. Kristoff wouldn't tell me to come out here if he knew someone else was here, right? I scanned my surroundings once more before undressing. The hot water felt good on my muscles, making me realize just how sore I was. I leaned my head back, looking to the sky as I ran my fingers through my hair, getting all the tangles and knots from it. Something brushed against my leg. I flinched then looked into the water. It had black curls, but that's all I could see. "I'm not getting eaten today." I kicked out and heard a grunt of pain come from something. No, it was someone. The fog cleared and I came face to face with him.

5

AN UNWANTED PROPOSAL

"What the fuck are you doing in here?" I shouted at the crimson eyed fae that led us here.

"I'm enjoying the hot springs, Your Grace," he said. Then smiled at me. I hated the way my body reacted to him. He swam closer to me, but I backed up until the small shore brushed against my back.

"You need to get out," I said, a stammer coating my words. "Now."

"Is that an order, Your Grace?" he asked, and I really needed to find out this man's name before I kept calling him other pronouns. His eyes pierced mine, but I noticed they never left my face. We were both naked, but he didn't make any move to look at my breasts.

"Who are you?" I asked.

"You already know who I am," he answered, keeping a short distance between us.

"Please tell me. I keep calling you 'He' or 'that male fae with crimson eyes.'" He laughed and I smiled.

"You love giving everything a name. Don't you, Your Grace?" His snarky question had me trying to wrap my head around how he knew an intimate fact about me. Why was he acting like he knew me? Then I looked deep into him. My powers came to life as I searched for this fae's name. Ash filled my mouth, fire flooded my veins, but I wasn't burning from pain. Magic was overwhelmingly addicting, like an endless pool of power that would not let me come up for air. I felt desire for him. My core heating, an ache developing deep inside of me to bond with him pulled me closer. It was a small kernel but it was there. His name floated into my mind and I didn't realize I had closed the distance between us until my nipples touched his chest. My hands were cupping his face, and our lips were a whisper away, and I spoke his name, "Blade."

"Queen Peech," he whispered my name back to me. "You're glowing."

"What?" I blinked the trance I was in away from my eyes then followed his gaze to the bright pink object floating between us. The ring breeches the surface until it was between us. I connected my gaze with his then backed away slightly, but his hands captured my wrist. "It can't be."

"It is. My name is Blade Feynard. Tomas, the late king, was my uncle."

"Making you Beaux's cousin. Which means?" I turned around, but the chain was tight around my neck and I realized that's because the ring was still floating behind me. It was the object telling me it was Blade. That this was the man, the royal fae that I had to marry to ensure peace. "I'm not sure I can do this."

"We don't have to do anything, Your Grace."

"How do you know all of this? Who sent you?" I turned to face him.

"Can I show you? It's easier than explaining it," he responded, and I nodded, letting his fingers brush against my temples. My skin coming to life under his touch. I felt sick that my body was responding to him the way it did Beaux. Why was I reacting to this man so strongly? Pain washed through me, my muscles tightening as I tried to douse the flames of desire coming to life within me. This was bad. My heart felt like it was twisting as thoughts of betrayal came to life. I was betraying Beaux. "Close your eyes, Your Grace."

I did, and as I let Blade into my head, I saw the second Beaux came to him in his dreams. Telling him that I would need Blade's help to bring peace to the realm. It was as clear as day. "You'll have to marry her, Bow. But don't push her into it. In time, she will trust you."

"How do you know this? Where are you?" Blade asked him.

"I'm dead, Blade," Beaux responded. His name copying the nickname he called his cousin. I saw the emotion take hold of Blade at the news of Beaux's death. "When she comes back to you with this ring around her neck, you'll know I'm speaking the truth because it will glow in your presence."

The vision faded and I blinked until I saw rubies staring at me intently. "Now you see the truth for yourself. He told me that I needed to offer myself to you as your consort. And I will, Your Grace. To honor him and to bring true peace between fae and humans."

It took me a few minutes to soak this revelation in, then I looked at Blade again. "What will happen when I give this to you?"

"I don't know," he answered, and I could tell he was speaking the truth. How can this be a way to honor him? Will I truly bring peace to the realm by marrying this fae? The questions were answered with Beaux's own words playing on repeat in my head.

I swallowed the emotion bubbling in my throat, unclasped he necklace from my neck then reached around Blade's neck, securing it. "Blade Feynard, will you do me the honor of becoming my king consort?"

Emotion coated every word I said, but the ring glowed brighter between us. Like I imagine the stars would look if I was close enough to touch them. Blade placed his hands on my shoulders then we closed the last of distance between us before he said. "Yes."

Our lips came together as fire erupted between us, a vibrant pink flame engulfing our bodies as we opened ourselves to each. His tongue clashing with mine, I wrapped my legs around his waist allowing his cock to line up with my entrance. My head fell backwards as I sank onto him. A moan of pleasure erupting between us. I wasn't sure how or why I was letting this man consume me. But then I saw him—Beaux's soul, his flame, reaching out to mine. Our fingers interlaced, and that's when I realized why the ring glowed. It was Beaux's essence. He chose Blade to take him into his body, so I could consummate the bond between us.

"Speak the vow," Blade's mouth moved, but Beaux's voice captured my attention. "Claim your twin flame before the fire dies out."

My eyes locked with Blade's, and in unison, we said, "I claim my twin flame. Mind, body, and soul." Magic erupted louder, and I felt our flames join as one. Blade's body rocked as he plunged in and out of me. My pussy clenching down on him as our mouths came together again. My skin was alive with power and I was on the edge. I could feel Blade coming with me. I clenched down as he filled me with his seed. Our moans drowned out with our lips locked.

Our breathing came in and out, our foreheads pressed together, and when I finally looked at him again, I saw them both. Beaux's horns were protruding from Blade's long black curls. His eyes were the perfect shade of red, and over his right pec was the scar that reminded me of Beaux's fatal wound.

"Look down, Your Grace." I followed his gaze to my right breast and saw it. The fae rose blossomed over my chest in red ink. "The symbol of my heritage." I looked at his chest then saw a five-pointed star with a halo around it. My palm pressed over it as his palm pressed over mine. "We're mated for life, Your Grace."

"How? I thought we had to perform the ceremony?"

"You just did," Kristoff's voice cut through our bubble like a blade cutting through bread. I didn't move from Blade's embrace as he was sort of blocking my naked chest from view. "You are the Goddess of all Fae, Your Grace. Which means you have the power to perform the marriage vows without a fae priest being present. Congratulations, Your Majesty."

Kristoff bowed in Blade's direction, and I couldn't help but pull the fae closer. I was married and it didn't feel wrong. Everything that happened felt right. "Blade?"

He looked at me then smiled as if he knew just what I was thinking. "Kristoff, if you'll excuse us, we need a little more time before rejoining the group."

"Newlyweds." Kristoff sighed then left us alone.

"Take me to the house," I whispered as he pulled out of me. "Make love to me and fill my womb with our heir." Words I never thought would leave my lips.

"As you wish, Your Grace."

I snapped awake. Sweat coating my skin as I tossed the sheets off of my body and went to the bathroom sink, turning the water on to splash my face. When I looked into the mirror, I pulled my shirt aside and saw no mark.

"It was just a dream," I whispered, clutching the ring dangling from the chain tighter. I looked at the faint glow. It appeared like it was beating. As if it were a heart. Matching the rhythm of my own organ. "Beaux, are you in there?"

It shone brightly. Okay, it could be a possessed ring but just to be sure. I cleared my throat and said, "Vibrate in my hand if you can hear me."

I waited a moment; it vibrated, and I gasped in shock. "Now two vibrates for yes and don't vibrate for no. Understand?" It vibrated twice in my palm. "Was that a vision?" Two vibrations. "So, you're telling me I need to marry your cousin who has the name Blade, looks like you, and make a baby with him?"

Yes. I sighed and then looked back at the ring. "Will your soul leave this ring and go into him?" Two vibrations. "I don't think I can do it, Beaux. We never got to even consummate our bond." The ring didn't move a muscle or trinket. Not sure what to call it. "Beaux, if I marry him, do I have to consummate the marriage?" Two vibrations.

How do I give myself to another, when my heart and soul remain with Beaux? I never got the chance to explore that level of intimacy with Beaux. It was always a choice for us to wait until after the chaos of war settled. When peace was finally won. Silent tears fell from my eyes as I hugged my knees to my chest. "I don't think I can go through with it. Gods be damned for taking you away from me. For bringing you to me when I needed you the most. Even when I didn't know it. Goddess be damned for making me love you. Then forcing me to lose you."

Sobs tore through my throat. I stayed there for some time, allowing myself to grieve. I needed to pull myself together. To be the queen that Klanstia and Itcha deserved. And to finally embrace my goddess self.

I let the ring hang from my neck again then went to the shower to wash the remnants of the dream from my body. After I was clean and put on fresh clothes, I secured my hair into a braid, my weapons on my belt, and went out into the hall. A wall of muscle hit me in the face or really just a chest. When I looked up, I caught the small grin that belonged to Blade.

“Good morning, Your Grace. Any good dreams?” What? Why was he asking me that? Could he sense it?

“What are you doing here?” I asked, and he quirked a dark brow before showing me the towel hanging over his shoulder. His black curls were still dripping with fresh water.

“Just came from the hot springs. You should really take a dip. I’ll even join you if you want some company.” The ring vibrated twice, but I didn’t want to acknowledge Beaux’s spirit encouraging me to sleep with his cousin.

“Blade.” He flinched backwards, confusion lining his brow.

"How do you know my name?" Blade was genuinely surprised. Then, quick as lightning, he had my blade pressed to my neck. "Tell me, Peech, how do you know my name?"

The ring vibrated so loud and glowed as bright as the sun. "I am the Goddess of all Fae. It isn't hard for me to find out," I snapped. His dark red eyes narrowed at me then he leaned forward, brushing his nose along my neck and inhaled deeply.

"We need to talk, Your Grace, and if you know my name, then you know what we must discuss," he whispered in my ear. My body betrayed me with the memory of the dream I had of us. Heat flooding my core as I felt my nipples harden, and I could smell lust and dare coming from him. He chuckled then I felt his fingers trace the line of my jaw, his thumb going along my bottom lip. He hummed in approval before stepping away, leaving me alone in the hall. I noticed he took my dagger with him.

I made my way down to the breakfast nook. A feast was laid out before me with biscuits and meats, poached eggs, and freshly squeezed orange juice. The other fae and my two guards were sitting around the table eating and talking. Jen had a smile on her face as she looked in Demetri's eyes. A look I was all too familiar with.

"Your Majesty." Jen and Demetri went to stand, but I waved them off.

"Not here. I'm going to eat. You two enjoy the down time." Then I grabbed a plate they had prepared for me and went to the back porch. I swiped a blanket from the closet that connected to the wash room and wrapped it around myself as I took a seat on the bench. My focus on the steam coming from the hot springs. How did a dream feel so real? When it came down to it, would I be able to marry him?

I took a bite of the biscuit, savoring the sweet butter and flaky dough, but I missed Connie's rosemary ones. My thoughts drifted to Patrice, praying she was still safe. I know Maya would protect her.

"May I join you?" Blade asked with a cup of steaming coffee in his hands. I nodded and he took a seat next to me on the bench, our thighs rubbing together. We were silent, but the tension was getting tighter, and if one of us didn't speak, I feel like the thread would snap any second. "I know you don't want to marry me." I didn't look at him. "You're still in mourning over my cousin and that's understandable. But perhaps, one day you will give me a chance."

"Blade." I caught his eyes looking at me intently. The desire to please adamant in his gaze. "I know that it is my duty to protect the realm. To bring true peace between Klansita and Iticha, but marrying you feels like betraying him." He nodded.

"Even when he is the one who told you to do it? And he has given you his flame to give to me. Wouldn't that be considered his form of blessing our union?" he asked, and I looked at the glowing ring around my neck. "Peech, I'm not saying you have to love me but," he moved to kneel in front of me, grabbing my hands in his, "marry me. Help me bring everlasting peace to us all.

"You sound just like King Tomas did. Another political arrangement." The words came out harsher than I intended. Blade physically flinched as If I hit him. My gaze looked past him. Beaux was playing matchmaker from beyond the grave, and I had to trust this was what was best.

"Your Grace, I do not intend on being your husband in name only. Nor do I wish for this just to be an arrangement."

"But that is what this is."

Blade sighed. "If we marry, I intend to give you anything and everything. You want to use me as your sword? Done. You want me to give you an heir then never touch you again, so be it. And if you want to burn the world down."

"You'll burn it?"

Blade's gaze burned into mine, a mix of hunger and admiration before he responded. "I'll be the match you light. Use me, Your Grace. For anything and everything."

"I don't want you as tool or weapon at my disposal, Blade. You're still a Fae. Do you think I am selfish? Or cruel? If so, then why are we proposing this marriage?"

"Not at all. But I wanted to be clear that I do not want to do anything without your expressed consent. I will only touch you when ask me to, and if you do not ask me to, I will wait."

"How long?"

"Eternity. Because you are worth it." His declaration reached the broken pieces of me, pulling them back into place. Not all of them.

The ring vibrated twice. I looked down at it. Then reached for the necklace unclasping it to pull the ring from it. The pink gem was so bright, it nearly blinded me. I closed my eyes and my palm around it. When I opened them again, I took his right hand and pushed the ring on his finger. It was now more masculine looking. Round with a smaller pink gems embellished around it. And in that moment, I knew Beaux had reached out from the veil to make it. Fae magic was still new to me, but alchemy didn't seem like it would be too difficult for a fae with dragon powers.

When my eyes met Blade's again, I swallowed the hard lump of emotion in my throat and gave him an answer, "Yes."

6

THE PROCLAMATION

"Are you sure this is a wise move, Your Majesty?" Jen asked as Demetri paced the small living space of my room. He'd been doing that since I told them about the engagement.

"It is what Beaux told me needed to be done," I responded, looking into her bright eyes. They were filled with a mix of sympathy and concern. Jen had always been the more empathetic of my generals. "When I went into the veil as the seer showed me the answers I'd been seeking, I saw Beaux. The ring I'd sent with him to the Otherworld was around his neck. He gave it to me after he'd blessed it. Beaux told me it would show me the man I needed to marry in order for there to finally be peace between humans and fae. A ceremony preformed under the eyes of the fates is what can do it."

"And Blade is of royal fae blood?" she asked.

I nodded.

"My Queen, I don't trust him," Demetri said, finally stopping his pacing to come sit with us at the small table next to the bed. "He was a soldier in the Klanstia army after all. A general."

Demetri was right. Blade was going to be killed because he was a general that had failed to complete some mission. They accused him of helping me. Jen gripped my hands then snatched them back thinking she had crossed the line. I grabbed hers and squeezed while saying, "I need you both to be at my side when I marry him."

"But those spots are reserved for those that have earned the honor of being next to you," Jen stated in surprise.

I looked between the two of them, letting go of one of Jen's hands to grasp the fidgeting hand of my other guard. "Then you two are perfect for the job."

After I broke the news to my two guards, it was time to speak with Kristoff again. Needing to know how soon I was to become a bride. I found the old fae rummaging through his kitchen cabinets, something boiling on the stove top. The steam filling the small room with the overwhelming smell of lemon and honey. Was he making tea?

"You'll need to drink this every night until your wedding night," he said without turning around to face me. There was something small in his right hand. A green herb that he crushed and sprinkled into the pot. The yellow liquid now at a rolling boil. I may not be a cook but I spent my younger days in the kitchen sneaking away with those rosemary butter biscuits to know what a rolling boil is.

"What is it?" I asked, peeking over his shoulder.

"Fertility tea," he responded without stopping his mixing.

"And why would I need that?"

"Because you have just come into your fae powers. I imagine you haven't had your monthly bleed since your journey began." I could see the question lingering in his eyes as he looked at me. He was right. I'd forgotten about my schedule. "Since you and your former lover did not consummate your bond, I know you are still a virgin."

I balked at that proclamation. It was true that I'd never had sex, but I was experienced. Between Mario and faeslayer, I had some inkling of what I liked and how to please a man. "That still doesn't answer my question. Why are making me fertility tea? I am not trying to get pregnant any time soon. Especially not with a war still going on."

Kristoff gave me a dubious look. "Listen. A child born of human and fae will have a stronger claim to the throne than that usurper Princess Plum. And as queen, you have a duty to provide an heir. For both realms."

"Okay, but I'm not going to have a child within the next year. I need to still learn how my powers work. To take back my queendom. I'm only marrying Blade because it is what Beaux advised me was the first step to true peace. Plus, I can name my sister as heir."

Kristoff shook his head in disappointment. "You have to stop doubting yourself, Your Majesty. You are not only the queen of the humans, but you are the goddess of all fae. We are your people too. Now, stop being so damned selfish."

Selfish? Did he just actually call me selfish? My hands curled into tight fist at my sides as rage consumed me. “And you are a disrespectful old man. I can’t believe you could even say that to me. I have just lost my home, my family, my twin flame, and my people. Everything that I thought I knew and the person I thought I was, was a lie. So forgive me if I want just a moment of peace where I do not have to be used to make everyone else’s lives easier.” I closed the distance between us, glaring into his silver eyes, and said, “I may be a queen and I may be this all powerful goddess, but I am still a person. I still have rights to what I choose to do with my body.

“Just because Beaux asked me to marry his cousin, does not mean I have to consummate the marriage. It does not mean that I have to give him an heir. I’m not some brood that is meant to be groomed and used for breeding.”

The floorboard creaked behind us, and a firm hand landed on my right shoulder, spinning me around with incredible strength. Two crimson eyes locked with mine. “I think you need to go for a walk, Your Grace.” It was Blade. “Now.”

I snarled something animalisctic at the fae then shrugged his hand off my shoulder and made a swift exit. The crisp air seemed to chill the heat from my skin. I made it to the edge of the hot springs in the back. The scent of lavender and soap filling me with ease. A small snapping of a twig had my senses on high alert. My fingers brushed the hilt of my daggers that I had strapped to my thighs. When the person took another step closer, I spun unsheathing my daggers in the process and struck.

Metal clinked against metal as Blade blocked my strikes. His eyes met mine, and I couldn't figure out what he was feeling. Did he come out here to scold me for the way I spoke to the seer? A dark brow of his rose in a challenge. Is he asking me to fight him? A small smirk played at the corner of his mouth. Lips that I could imagine pressing against my skin. Heat pooled in my lower belly, but I shook those feelings away pushing backwards until there was a good two feet distance between us.

"What do you want?" I asked.

He shrugged. "I know you're pissed. Instead of taking it out on Kristoff, use me."

Use me. Two words that could mean so many different things. Blade closed the distance between us in one long stride. His sandalwood and cinnamon scent washing over me as my knees bucked. I was ensnared by the intensity of his gaze, and the dream I had about him came back to the forefront of my mind. Would it feel that good in real life? Will I enjoy being fucked by him? Or having him taste me the same way Beaux did?

"Yes, Your Grace." I blinked at his words. Did I speak those thoughts allowed? His eyes slowly scrutinized me from head to toe. Slowing on the valley between my breast. The curves of my hips and then the apex of my thighs. Heat pooled between my legs when his tongue licked his bottom lips. It was as if he was imagining me as his next meal. I swallowed and then shifted in my spot. Blade met my gaze again then reached out to brush his knuckles along my cheek. "I will make it feel good, Your Grace. And I will only do what you ask me to do. I'm a soldier."

"What does that have to do with anything?" I asked.

He smirked then leaned forward as if to kiss me, but instead, he whispered in my ear, "It means I know how to follow orders." Then his face pressed into my neck. He inhaled my scent and my hands wanted to drop my weapons and touch him. Blade chuckled, his breath sending heat coursing throughout my body. "I can smell your lust for me, Your Grace."

My nose involuntarily inhaled his scent. It smelled like him, only there was another aroma starting to overpower it. Can fae smell that? "How do you know?"

My question came out as a whisper. Blade's tongue darted out, the tip of it delicately moved across my neck along my most sensitive vein and a moan escaped me. His lips sucked on my ear, and my daggers dropped to the grass as my hands went to his hips and pulled his body flush against mine. I could not only smell his arousal but feel his hard length pressing against my belly. "I think we need to separate before I fuck you in that hot spring, Your Grace."

When his playful eyes met mine again, something clicked in me. Oh gods, it wasn't just my dream but our dream. I went to slap him but he gripped my wrist and spun me around. My chest hit his back. His hand wrapped around my throat while the other had my arm bent in a strange position. If I moved, my shoulder would be dislocated. His lips grazed my ear again and he whispered, "I was there too, Your Grace. I promise if we consummate our marriage, it will feel ten-thousands time better than our sex dream."

"How can we share a dream?" I was panting with need now. Regardless of how controlling he was over me, my pussy was throbbing with need. "We aren't anything to one another. I hadn't agreed to marry you until after."

Blade chuckled again. "You don't get it, do you?"

"Obviously. In case you forgot, I'm new to this being fae thing." His grip loosened and he created space between us. I inhaled a calming breath, but when I looked at him again, he was shirtless. "What are you doing?"

His pants went next and I gaped as his erection jutted out. Blade was long and thick. From what I could see, he was bigger than his cousin. In a blink of an eye he was naked and in front of me. "It is okay to seek release, Your Grace. Tell me what you need and you will have it. Want to wait to taste me until we are married, then so be it, but I'm going into the hot spring with or without you."

He walked past me and I didn't have to convince myself otherwise. Gods, how the fuck am I so turned on? I stared at Blade's pert ass, my pussy still throbbing and then undressed. When I made it to the edge of the water, Blade was sitting stroking his length. I sat across from him. I expected his eyes to drift from my face but they didn't. I watched him slowly run his hand up and down his shaft then my hands moved to my thighs.

"Do you want to touch me, Your Grace?" It was a simple yes or no question, but I couldn't figure what I wanted. "Command me."

But that was it. I didn't feel like being the leader right now. I needed to lose control, not maintain it. Being that all my decisions as a queen of late has led to the loss of many lives, I had no right to command this man.

Blade seemed to read my thoughts because he was in the water wading over to me in the next second. I opened my legs for him. His mouth at the perfect height. When I looked at him again, I whispered, "I don't want to be in charge, Blade."

He smiled at me. It was with pity but with understanding. "Then I have your permission to touch you? To taste you?"

I reached out to him. His beard was soft and I wondered what it was going to feel like as he pressed that sinful tongue of his to my clit. Without words, I gripped the back of his head, positioned my thighs over his shoulders and pressed my pussy to his face. His tongue darted out, licking through my wetness before he sucked my clit.

My back arched, the steam from the hot spring mixed with the cold winter air causing sweat to bead on my skin. I felt my breast become full and my nipples hardened. Blade's eyes met mine as he continued to lick me. Sucking and teasing before one of his hands moved to my entrance, pushing one finger in first. He was sucking my clit, pushing that single finger in and out at a slow pace. Then, he added another and my hips started to move on their own. Soon, I was fucking his tongue and his fingers. But my body needed more. Wanted to feel his length inside of me.

"Ride my tongue, Peech. Let go." Blade was coaxing my orgasm forward. He added another finger and nibbled on my clit. My grip on his hair was hard and my hips picked up pace and I felt the tingle in my lower spine. My climax was coming and then Blade stick just the tip of his finger into my ass. It was a small burn but mixed with the pleasure of his tongue, sent me over. Waves of pleasure washed over me as I rode it out on his fingers.

When he looked at me again, my climax was dripping from his beard. His lips were swollen and glossed over. I watched his tongue dart out as he licked the taste of me off of them. That movement almost made me come again. I slide into the pool, my arms wrapping around his neck and before I knew it, my lips were on his. It was a small kiss but then it turned blazing. My tongue pushed between his lips and he opened to me. I could feel his erection pressing against my belly and the need to have him was taking over.

I reached between us and gripped him in my hand, moving to put his tip at my entrance. But he stopped me. "As much as I want to fuck that tight little pussy, now is not the right time." I gave him a dubious look and he sighed. "You're a virgin, Peech. I need to make sure it feels good for you."

"If it is anything like the dream, then I'm sure it will." I moved the tip of his cock again and then teased it along the folds of my pussy. We were in the water, but I knew I was wet from my climax. "Please, Blade. Fuck me."

I could feel his restraint was starting to loosen. His lips were on mine again, but I needed to make sure

I had his consent before I pushed him inside of me. “Are you going to fuck me?”

His crimson eyes were alight with desire and he nodded but then backed away from me. “I’m going to fuck you, Peech, but not right now.”

“Why?” I didn’t expect the crack in my voice when I asked.

“Because your first time will be as my wife. You are not use to the arousal fae feel and how demanding the need to mate is, but I do.” He was telling me he had been with others before. “I have had all my life to control the lust, but you are still new. Innocent.”

I’d hardly call what we did innocent. The thought played in my head and I swam closer to him. His back was at the pool’s edge, and I reached out to cup his cheeks. There was a pleading reflecting in his eyes, and I knew I needed to back off. He was doing this for me. Because he cared enough about me to wait. To give me my release even if it meant he didn’t get his.

I leaned in and kissed him softly, whispering in his ear, “Thank you, Blade.”

“I only want to make sure that you are with me because it’s what you want, not some carnal urge.

Right now, you will say yes. And even after the first twenty times you will. But then, once the haze of lust fades, you might regret it. I don't want you to regret being my wife or my mate. Please understand it's not because I'm not attracted to you. I also know that you're mourning your life. The man you thought was your twin flame. The loss of your home and your family." A single tear left my eye and he wiped it away. The haze of lust fading as strong emotions for this fae came over. Blade was protecting me. "I will not allow you to sabotage yourself, Peech." I looked down in shame, but he gripped my chin gently and leveled my gaze with his. "Use me, Peech. For your anger, I will be the punching bag. For your lust, I will be yours to fuck in whatever way you will have me. If you need to hate someone, hate me because then I know you feel something for me." I blinked at his proclamation, and my respect for this man—for my fiancé—grew tenfold. "I will wait for you forever if I have to, because I'm in this till death."

Gods, I needed to get away from him right now. "Blade." I didn't know what else to say, but I let him hold me. The way his body relaxed against mine told me he understood what I was trying to say. I rested my head on his chest, listening to the beating of his heart as we just stayed with each other in the silence.

7

DINNER PARTY

"My name is Henre Stainfall, I am from the northern side of Klanstia where many fae like me live." The other four fae generals introduced themselves. We'd spent two nights and one day—now two, counting today—and I was only just getting to know the rest of the fugitives. Henre had a bald head and bright green eyes. He was tall but slender and his scent was like a wildflower.

They all had showered and slept. I still wasn't sure how things kept magically appearing. The smell of roasted potatoes and seared meat had my stomach growling with hunger.

But then something else caught my senses. I knew Blade had entered the room the second his sandalwood scent caught my nose. My thighs squeezed together as arousal started to stir. Gods, what was wrong with me? Did all fae lose control of their lust around their mate?

"Sorry, I'm late," he said, then took the chair right next to me. Our thighs brushed together, and I cursed the clothes that kept our bare skin from touching. The room suddenly got hot, and Blade leaned in, pressed his nose to my neck, and inhaled long and slowly. I turned my head to meet his heated gaze with mine, and our noses brushed slightly.

Curiosity was a fickle thing in this moment. I had a thousand and one questions that needed answering. Was Blade the right fae to teach me? I leaned in, wanting to press my lips to his again, but someone cleared their throat, breaking our little bubble.

"I hear congratulations are in order," the red-hair female fae said, Blair, I think was her name. I looked at her and expected to find truth in her words, but there was nothing but hate gleaming in her pink eyes. What kind of fae was she? Why did she look like she wanted to claw my face off?

"Thank you, Blair," Blade said.

"Tell me, Your Majesty, how was your dip in the hot springs?" The water I sipped on nearly choked me with the surprise of her question. My throat burned as I coughed.

"Are you okay, Your Majesty?" Jen asked from the other side of me.

I nodded. "Just went down the wrong pipe," I responded, my voice sounding hoarse. There was a brief silence as I gathered my composure. This time when I drank, it went down with ease.

"Everyone eat before our queen dies of thirst," Blade momentarily commanded, and soon the moving of dishes filled the room. Side conversations buzzed around us, including whispered words between Blair and Blade. I didn't try to eavesdrop, but being fae enhanced all my senses, including hearing. I hid the devious act while chewing on some potatoes and focusing on my plate.

"Did you tell her?" Blair whispered.

"Not yet," Blade answered.

"You shouldn't be marrying her, B. You're mine, remember?" Blair snarled. What the hell is she talking about?

"Not anymore. She asked me to marry her and I said yes. I'm not yours anymore." So, Blade was Blair's mate, and my proposal ended their relationship. No wonder she looked like she wanted me dead.

I felt Blade tense. My eyes drifted to Blair's bicep, the table hiding the rest of her arm, but by the back-and-forth motion, even if it's slow, I could tell what she was doing to him. "Should I remind you of how good it feels to be with me?" she whispered.

"Stop it," Blade growled, and he pushed her hand away.

I watched from the corner of my eye as Blair leaned in and tried to inhale his scent. Blade shot to his feet, asking to be excused to the bathroom. Blair got up to chase him down the hall. Should I go after them?

"Don't let her do that," Jen whispered, and I looked at her in question. "He's your fiancé. Your soon-to-be husband. She needs to know you won't let her touch what's yours."

She was right. I excused myself from the table and rounded the corner. Blair was knocking on the door, trying to turn the obviously locked handle. Her side profile was beautiful. Fiery red hair, curved athletic build. The pants and shirts were slightly too big for her frame, but she pulled the look off well. I was given a dress that was tight around my waist and didn't keep the tops of my cleavage from showing. Nothing a queen should be wearing. They also didn't give me any undergarments to wear, not that I was complaining.

I stopped on the wall behind her, leaned back, and crossed my arms. Blair turned to face me. Her sneer was evident. Then her eyes welled up with tears.

"He was supposed to marry me. Then you took him." She cried.

"I didn't know," I responded, sympathy coating my tone.

She moved to close the distance, then sighed. "He'll be good to you. Just don't break his heart. Or I will kill you."

Blair was gone and around the corner before I could process the threat. I approached the door and knocked lightly. Heavy footfalls came, and the door jerked open. "I said back the fuck off."

Blade took a second to recognize me. "Do you want me to leave?"

He stepped out of the bathroom and then gripped my hand, ushering me upstairs, down the hall, and into his bedroom. The door closed, and I heard the lock move into place. "Please stay away from me while I answer your questions. I need to stay in control, and if your scent hits me, I don't think I can maintain it."

I looked around the room then grabbed the small chair from his side table and walked to the farthest corner of the room to sit. Blade turned to face me. His button-down black shirt fit him nicely. In the light, his red eyes started to burn. His curly black locks came in waves, framing his beautiful face.

"Stop looking at me like that," he growled.

"Like what?" I squeezed my thighs tightly, his scent causing arousal to blossom deep inside of me.

He shook his head and started to speak, "When two fae commit themselves to one another, there are moments when uncontrollable lust takes over until they perform the mating act. When we agreed to marry each other, that was the first step. Allowing me to taste you was only the beginning."

My insides burned with the memory of his tongue. "What about Blair? She said you were hers. What happened? Why didn't you tell me?"

He stopped pacing then looked at me. "Blair and I fooled around a little, but we never had sex. Kissing and empty words. She thought I was going to propose to her after the war, but I knew that I wasn't. When she learned of our engagement, I guess it broke her heart."

"You guess? She looked like she wanted to claw my eyes out at the dinner table." He smiled then it fell. "Blade, how can I make this ache go away?"

He visibly swallowed, but I saw the truth in his eyes. "It won't subside until we mate. And even then, I don't think I'll ever stop craving you."

Gods, this man could talk the pants off anyone.

"No. Not anyone, just my mate." I leaned back in surprise. "No, I can't read your mind, but your expressions give away your thoughts."

"With that ring, with Beaux's blessing, is a part of him inside of you? He was supposed to be my twin flame. Is that why I feel this burning ache to be near you now? To be with you. Protect you?" The questions kept coming and he waited for me to finish. "And when we are married and make love, will it actually be love or lust? How do I know this isn't just another mistake? Why do I feel like I can trust you completely?"

Blade blinked once then took a seat at the edge of his bed. "Beaux gifted his blessing to me. That means that your twin flame bond with him was relinquished to me. I'd never heard of it happening before outside of lore and legend. There was a passage I remember reading about when I was a little boy. How one of the first faes had to gift his twin flame spark to another so that his mate would live a life of love and happiness. He had died protecting her before they could consummate their bond. Until now, I didn't know that it could happen."

I stood and made my way over to him. His hands gripped my hips, and he pulled me down on top of him. Our lips didn't meet but our eyes did. He rolled us and then he stepped back. I immediacy missed the weight of him. "The reason you want to fuck me is because I carry that spark inside of me. It's the reason you two couldn't resist coming together the way you did."

"But we never had sex," I whispered.

He smiled. "I know."

"So will it be love?"

Blade came to me and neeled at my feet to meet my eyes. "I don't know what love feels like, Peech. But I promise once we feel it, we will make it known to the world."

I cupped his face in my hands and leaned down to kiss him. It was soft and then turned feverish. Blade pressed into me on the bed, the evidence of his arousal pressing into me through the seam of his pants. I wrapped my legs around him as he bunched up the skirts of my dress exposing me to the air. I shamelessly moved my hips, rubbing my clit against his pants because the need to climax again was burning inside of me.

Blade's tongue met mine, thrust for thrust as his hips moved against mine. I wanted to feel him inside of me. Filling me with his seed. I needed to taste him as he tasted me. I rolled us over, gripping his wrist in one of my hands to pin them above his head. My lips grazed his jawline then down his chest. I skillfully unbuttoned his shirt, a trail of kisses following until I landed at his waist band. His belt was next and I pulled it loose from his pants before binding his hands together behind his back.

Blade didn't say a word as he let me take control. This was something I wanted to do. I needed to know what I was doing to him. I pulled his pants down to his ankles and then licked the tip of his cock. My tongue traced the vein underneath as I wrapped one hand around his shaft, the tips of my fingers barely touching. I took him into my mouth, all the way to the back of my throat and relax my jaw. Sucking and licking.

"Fuck." He groaned.

I couldn't help but feel pride as I continued to move up and down. My hand matching the rhythm. Blade's hips started to move and I let him, keeping him deep as he thrust in and out. His pace started to thicken. Tears burned in my eyes but I didn't move and I reached out to caress his swollen balls, one finger teasing his puckered hole. It was enough to send him over the edge. Hot seed spilled into my throat and I swallowed, relishing in the cinnamon taste of him.

I moved on top of him until my pussy was over his semi-hard cock. My hips moved and I could feel my clit throb harder and need for him grow stronger. "Blade, please."

"Unbind my hands," he demanded, and I did. I could feel him getting hard again. "You want me to fuck your tight little pussy?"

"Yes," I moaned as he removed my dress. Clamping one nipple into his mouth. I pulled his shirt off and we were naked together again. Only this time, nothing was holding us back. The truth was evident. I needed to have sex with him just as much as he needed to be with me. Our souls longed to be united as one.

"Are you sure?" His voice was soft and I looked at him, all movements stopped. I reached between us and let his tip push against my entrance. "Peech, for the love of the gods, I need your consent."

"You have it." I pushed down until he was completely inside of me. It burned a little as my body stretched to fit him. Gods, it felt right. This is what I needed. What I wanted from him in the hot springs. "Make love to me, Blade."

He moved quickly as I ended up on my back. He pulled out and pushed back in. Slow and sensual at first. "Harder."

Blade claimed my lips. Moving in and out of me at a speed I thought was going to take my breath away. My heels dug into his ass, nails dug into his back as I moved closed to him. We moved positions, I straddled him, moving my hips in rhythm to match his thrust. Our bodies moved in perfect harmony. Souls connecting as one. My eyes met his, one of his hands gripped my hip the other reaching between us to stimulate my clit. His thrust became stronger and I new he was close.

I could feel him swelling inside of me. "Come with me, Peech."

I kissed him hard and fast. Letting go the moment he spilled himself inside of me. Our eyes locked, and when I blinked, I saw our flames coming together as one.

"So that's what I've been missing out on all these years." We laughed as I cuddled close to him.

"There's so much more, but you're not ready for it," he said, and I looked up at him. "How are you feeling?"

"Sore. But I want to do it again," I admitted, feeling the heat rise in my cheeks.

Blade smiled and I noticed his dimples appear. "I meant on the inside."

I knew what he was asking. There was no lying to him or myself. "I feel like I finally found the man I'm meant to spend the rest of my life with. I miss Beaux, but being with you, that spark he blessed you with, it's almost like he was here with us."

Blade looked around. "Are you saying Beaux's spirit watched us fuck?"

I playfully smacked his chest. "You know what I meant."

He took my hand and kissed the back of it. "I agree with you." I raised a brow and he sat up, pulling me to straddle him again. I felt him start to get hard again. "I finally found the woman I'm going to spend the rest of my life with." It can't be this easy, right? Beaux, if you're somehow nearby, you've got to tell me this is real. "You're thinking about him, aren't you?" Blade asked. "How did you know?"

"Because a sprinkle of sadness and guilt reflects in your eyes. It's okay to still want him, Peech. He was your first love." He gripped my chin to spear me with a look so full of admiration I could melt. "I'm going to be your last."

8

AN UNEXPECTED LESSON

"After the ceremony today, you four will need to journey to Klansita. There, you will find the fae crown. With the ring," Kristoff gripped my right hand, lifting to show my old engagement ring to the room, "and the crown, Queen Peech will have the ability to command every fae in this realm. No one will be able to disobey her." Kristoff's eyes pierced into mine as if he was trying to warn me.

"But doesn't she already have that power as the goddess of all fae?" Jen asked. Yes, tell me Kristoff, how come I can't do that now? Oh wait, because I haven't mastered my new powers.

"Queen Peech is still new to having magic. It takes time to hone the skills you weren't born with. If there was more time, I would teach her but alas, Princess Plum cannot continue to reign terror over Iticha. So, goddess," he looked back at me, "you will need to use caution when wearing the items as I'm sure you remember from the last time how intoxicating they can be."

Kristoff's warning echoed in my mind, a stark reminder of the intoxicating allure of the crown and ring. I closed my eyes, envisioning how this could play out. As I held the artifacts, I felt the weight of their power thrumming beneath my fingertips, beckoning me with promises of unmatched strength and dominion. My heart pounded with a mix of excitement and dread. I envisioned using this power to usher in an era of peace, to right the wrongs of my past, and to protect those I loved. Yet, the fear of losing myself, of succumbing to the same hubris that had doomed so many before me, gnawed at my resolve.

Yes. I commanded Beaux to leave me and as much as he resisted, he couldn't stop his body from reacting. "I want there to be an anchor. Someone that can remind me of who I am and what the purpose of this crown and ring are. Someone like you." I turned to look at Blade.

"But I am fae too," Blade stated. "I would be under your control as well." Of course he doesn't understand. How could he?

"Could I speak with Kristoff alone, please?" I asked the others, and just as per usual, Demetri and Jen left without question. Blade gave me a dubious look. "You too." I expected him to give me grief but he nodded, placed a gentle kiss on my cheek, and exited the room. Once I knew we were alone, I walked over to the bay window that looked out at the snow-covered plains. Thoughts of Patrice filter through my mind as I try to remember if she'd ever seen snow before. Then, I remembered that it doesn't snow back home.

A heavy sigh escaped me as Kristoff came up to my right side and said, "Your sister is safe. Maya has fiercely protected her this entire time, but I know she weighs heavily on your mind and on your heart. That is why you will fail in your mission to save the realm." I snapped my attention and faced the old fae.

"I will not fail."

"You will if you can not control those human emotions."

"Human emotions? What does love and worry for my sister and my people have to do with my mission? It's because of those strong human emotions that I am motivated to succeed." My tone was growing louder as rage coursed through my veins.

"This is exactly what I feared, Peech. Look at you?" I followed his gaze, noting an ethereal glow around my closed fist. "You're letting your emotions control every decision you make. That is also why you were quick to mate with Blade. Once you learned that your lost love's twin flame spark was inside of him, you just could not control the lust."

I physically stepped back. His words an invisible punch to my gut.

My mouth was agape. Words hovered on the tip of my tongue, but nothing came out. We stared at each other in silence, neither of us wanting to risk turning this conversation into something disrespectful or unnecessary. After a few moments, my anger faded, and I turned back to Kristoff. "I understand that you are just trying to advise me, but there is nothing that would ever make me erase the way I feel about my family. My people."

"Even if it means you will kill them?" he asked, and I flinched at the question. Physically stepped away from him as if his words slapped me in the face. "Because if you do not listen to me and follow my instructions word for word, step by step, Iticha will be wiped out and everyone you know and love will be gone."

Kristoff's serious tone and dark stare told me he was serious. "I know it may seem like I'm just trying to twist your emotions into doing as I say, but I truly wish to see peace." His withered eyes went soft and for the first time since meeting him, I could see the weight of his gift. Kristoff has seen all the outcomes. His power is just as dangerous as my own.

There were two options at this point. First, turn on my heel, gather up my companions and get the hell out of there. Or second, listen to what he has to say because he is a seer and probably knows what he is talking about. "I will hear you out. But when I make my final decision, you must respect it."

He nodded. I followed him to the round table and took my seat across from him. Kristoff folded his legs over one another then placed his clasped hands in his lap. "I will tell you the story of your father and his beloved daughter Lasir."

"The goddess for which I get my powers?" I asked and he nodded.

"Lasir was always curious as a child. Looking down at the humans, wondering what their purpose was. Who created them? And why were they born lesser than her and her family?" Kristoff adjusted his position, shifting in his seat and continued. "She would visit us often. The fae realm of Klanstia and us. One day, when she was a young woman, equivalent to twenty-three human years, she met a human male and instantly fell in love. He courted her as he would any other female in Iticha. Henry Whittington, your father was the Prince of Iticha at the time he met Lasir. They'd met during an underground illegal fae cage fighting match. This was a frequent place for her to visit. Henry was there one evening, trying to convince his guard which I think the young soldier was named Booth."

My heart stabbed in pain at the memory of him.

"Yes. Booth had protected your family since he turned eighteen years of age. That night, was his first night on the job. Your father insisted he fight. While your father prepared to fight the next contestant, Lasir overheard a plot to kill him. The fae fighter was working for a young prince—Tomas Feynard. He was going to stab him with a tip laced with viper venom. Only it was a lethal dose. Lasir, being the goddess she is, intervened and took the fighter's place." I blinked at the consequence of this history lesson. "That's how you and Beaux first met, isn't it?"

"Yes. Only we met before the fight, but we faced off with one another." After Mario tried to assault me. Worst decision of my life that man.

"After the cage fight, they met in Henry's room. Lasir was checking on him after she had knocked him out. And even with a black eye, she fell for him. The spark was there between the two of them, but a relationship between a goddess and a human was impossible. Forbidden. It didn't stop their courtship. They would love one another in secret. Months went on, and they met in secret at night. Messages left in coded letters, late-night swims, and picnics in the fields. Lasir had not told your father what she was. And your father was also keeping a secret from her." Kristoff sighed as if this next memory would be painful.

"Your father and Lasir gave in to their attraction. Making love underneath a blanket of stars. But their post-coital bliss was interrupted when Naxian came down in a thunder of clouds. He went to strike Henry, but Lasir stopped him, begging for his life. Now, Naxian, being the arrogant and prideful god he is, grew angry at seeing his daughter on her knees for a human. A lesser life-form. So what did he do?" Kristoff shook his head, and I started to think that he had been a witness to all this. Perhaps being a seer is just as much of a curse as it is a blessing.

"Naxian was not a forgiving god. He was vengeful. After that night, Lasir was locked back inside of her home and she would never be able to leave until Henry breathed his last breath. Lasir was heartbroken but even more so when she felt you blooming to life within her womb six weeks later."

"What?" I asked. "But, Lasir isn't my mother."

Kristoff's eyes softened when he looked at me. "Your grandfather is Naxian, and when he found out about you, he gave Lasir two choices: get rid of you or transfer your essence to Henry's wife. Lasir didn't know her beloved Henry was married until the night she found out about you. She had to see it for herself and that's when Naxian let her go to him. Henry was inside of his bed chamber, awaiting the arrival of his new bride for their consummation. She confronted him and although it broke her heart, she still couldn't imagine letting you go. So, Lasir waited until Henry and his beautiful bride were finished. The transference ritual was painful for Lasir but not for your mother. But Lasir accepted that you would be loved and cared for by your father and his wife.

"The weeks following, Lasir grew depressed. Neglected her duties. Her light was starting to dim. Her brother had gone off on his own adventure with their uncle, Cain. When Lasir's mother finally came to see her. Valexian was the Goddess of Life and Creation. She could gift life and take it away. Create and control the environment. That day she offered her daughter reprieve by saying Lasir's memories could be wiped clean. That way she would never have to think of the human prince or you again. It would take away her pain and her suffering."

I blinked a couple times, feeling something wet on my cheeks and realized I was crying. "My grandparents hated me. They wanted me dead."

"Oh, my sweet child, they did what they thought was best for their daughter."

"Bullshit. Anyone who uses that excuse is a pathetic piece of shit. You don't suggest killing your grandchild because your child made a decision."

"I know. But just as your powers are controlled by your emotions, so were Lasir's. All the fae under her control were about to break into a civil war. Her hatred fueled every fae in the realms. Your grandparents needed her to get control again. Lasir agreed to the ceremony but with all that power, it needed to be put into something. Only objects blessed by both Naxian and Valexian would be strong enough to hold the Goddess of Fae's powers. The ceremony went swiftly and the objects were stored safely in the vaults until they weren't.

"Tomas Feynard and your great-uncle Cain became acquainted. The fae prince didn't know it at the time, but he was a pawn. Once Cain had the fae crown and the ring used to contain Lasir's powers, he gave them to Tomas telling him that if he failed in the mission, then Cain would kill him. You know what happens next because you lived it." Kristoff finished his story then stood to stretch, whispering something to an invisible creature. Shuffling sounded in the kitchen, and then, minutes later, a tea tray appeared between us.

"Do you have little invisible creatures working for you?" I asked.

"You mean to tell me you can't see them?" he asked, and I shook my head no, scanning the room. Kristoff sipped on his tea and sighed. "Well, when they want you to see them, you will."

"What are they?"

"Sprites. They only show themselves when they trust you. Guess you haven't earned it yet."

"Anyways, what does my family history have to do with right now?" I took the tea that was offered to me. Add some sugar and cream. It was lemony with a hint of mint.

"Because you will have to do the same thing your mother did if you want to save the realms." I froze for a moment, processing what he said. "You will need to stripe yourself of human emotions in order to not let the powers infused into the objects overtake you."

"So, I have to become a shell?" I sipped on my tea again, welcoming the warmth coating my throat.

Kristoff set his tea cup down then leaned forward to look into my eyes deeply to answer. "You need to dehumanize yourself. Only a full-fledged Goddess of Naxian's blood will be able to control that much power." "But what about my sister? I will not feel my love for her?" Kristoff shook his head side to side. "What happens if I refuse?"

9

HAND FASTING CEREMONY

White lace fell in waves over my legs. The tight bodice highlighted the curves of my torso, covering my breast. I hardly recognized myself. My hair fell in auburn curls down my back contrasting beautiful with the white dress. “You look beautiful, Your Majesty.”

“Jen, while we are in closed quarters, I insist you call me Peech,” I reminded her.

“Right.” I met her bright gaze through my reflection. She of course dressed in a ceremonial general’s uniform. Still unsure how Kristoff managed to acquire that. I suspect his invisible friends helped. Jen’s sleek black locks were braided tightly at the back of her hair. The dark blue of her tunic highlighted her features perfectly. Golden lace seams showed her status and her pants were neatly tucked into her black boots. Her sword was fastened to her hip. Jen was made to be a general.

"Jen," I started, turning to face her. I gripped her hands in mine. "Thank you for standing by my side."

"Of course. It is my honor."

"No, Jen Josalen, it is mine."

We left my chambers to meet everyone out in the main living area. The ceremony was small being that Demetri and Jen stood at my side while the other four fae stood with Blade. Kristoff took his spot at the center of the make shift alter. I hadn't seen Blade in two days as it was customary for separation before the exchanging of vows. During that time, Jen and Demetri had stayed with me. Bringing me food, talking, and it was nice being in a peaceful place. There was no threat of war or death. Of course I thought of Patrice, but Kristoff reassured me that Maya was keeping her safe and I could feel it.

A soft chiming of bells had me blinking as I rounded the corner. I could feel my fingers digging into

Jen's bicep as a wave of nerves threatened to take hold of every muscle. But as soon as Blade's crimsons eyes met mine, I only saw him. The look of admiration, desire, respect, and unspoken promises captured me. Pulled me towards him. My hands found their way to his. I felt small standing in his presence. "You look beautiful, Your Grace."

"You too," I whispered. He smiled, revealing both dimples.

Standing in the cozy warmth of our small living room, I felt the magic in the air as Kristoff, the Seer Fae, began the ceremony. The flickering candles cast a soft glow on the walls, and the scent of incense mingled with the fresh flowers adorning the makeshift altar. Blade's hand was warm in mine, our fingers intertwined with a silken ribbon, symbolizing our union. Kristoff's voice, melodic and ancient, called upon the elements to bless us—earth for stability, air for clarity, fire for passion, and water for love.

"Blade, standing here with you, I am overwhelmed by the journey that brought us to this moment. In you, I have found not just a partner, but a soul intertwined with mine. We have faced trials that would break others, yet through it all, your unwavering strength and gentle heart have been my anchor.

“Today, I vow to stand by your side, not just in moments of triumph, but in the depths of darkness too. I promise to be your shield, your confidant, and your unwavering support. Together, we will face any challenge, knowing that our love is the greatest power we possess.

“As I place this ring upon your finger, know that it is not just a symbol of our union, but a testament to the adventures we will embark upon, the battles we will fight, and the power that will sustain us through it all. With you, I am home. With you, I am whole. I am your wife, Blade, now and always."

"Peech, from the moment our paths crossed, I knew my life would never be the same. Your courage, wisdom, and boundless compassion have not only saved me countless times but have also shown me the true meaning of love and partnership.

“Today, I vow to stand by you through every storm and every dawn. I promise to be your warrior and your sanctuary, to share in your dreams, and to support you in all your endeavors. No matter what challenges lie ahead, I will be your steadfast companion, your shield against the darkness, and your anchor in turbulent times.

“With this ring, I seal my promise to you, not just as my beloved, but as the one I will honor, cherish, and fight for every day of our lives. In you, I have found my true home, my heart, and my greatest adventure. I love you, Peech, now and forever."

Blade’s confession of love took me by surprise. I did not know he felt that strongly for me. Would I ever feel the same?

As we exchanged our vows, my heart swelled with emotion, each word a promise of our future together. The simple gold rings we slid onto each other’s fingers felt like the perfect embodiment of our eternal bond. With a final blessing from Kristoff, our union was sealed, and the room seemed to hum with the energy of our love and the blessings of the spirits.

The ceremony went quicker than I anticipated but the evening was here. And as per tradition, Blade and I would remain in our room until the second sunrise after the last vow was spoken. With my eyes covered by the soft blindfold Blade had gently tied around my head, I felt a mix of excitement and curiosity. His hand was warm and steady as he guided me through the house, his voice a soothing murmur in my ear. The scent of candles and flowers teased my senses, hinting at the surprise he had meticulously prepared. When he finally stopped and removed the blindfold, I blinked in amazement. The living room had been transformed into a romantic paradise. Candles flickered softly, casting a warm, golden glow over the room. Flowers were everywhere, their vibrant colors and sweet fragrance creating an enchanting atmosphere.

At the center of it all was a small table set for two, and my heart skipped a beat when I saw the plate of rosemary butter biscuits—my absolute favorite. Blade had remembered. Tears of joy welled up in my eyes as I turned to him, his face lit with a tender smile. "I remembered you said these were your favorite," he said softly, pulling me into a loving embrace. The intimate dinner that followed was perfect, filled with laughter, whispered promises, and the deep connection we shared. It was the perfect prelude to the night ahead, setting the stage for our new life together.

Sitting together in the dimly lit room, the warmth of the candles casting a soft glow around us, I felt a deep connection with Blade. He took my hand gently, his eyes reflecting the pain of old wounds. "I never told you the full story of how I lost my parents," he began, his voice heavy with emotion. "I was away on a training mission with Beaux. When I returned, our home was nothing but ash. My parents…they were just dust in the wind. I never told anyone else. You are the first," he whispered.

My heart ached for him, and I squeezed his hand, offering silent support. "I know what it's like to lose everything," I said softly. "I found my mother dead one morning. My father…he died of a broken heart not long after. But I later discovered it wasn't just heartbreak. Beaux's half-brother poisoned them. It was undetectable."

Blade's eyes widened in shock and sorrow. "I'm so sorry, Peech. I had no idea."

He hesitated before asking, "What about your sister, Patrice?"

A bittersweet smile crossed my face as I re-membered. "My favorite memory is sitting in the li-brary with her, snacking on rosemary biscuits and read-ing books. Those moments were so precious." Tears welled up in my eyes as Kristoff's words came flood-ing back. "Kristoff told me I would have to give up my humanity to control the powers of the fae crown and ring." Blade pulled me into his arms, his embrace strong and comforting. "No matter what happens, I will protect Patrice. She's my family now, too." His words, filled with love and determination, broke down the last of my defenses. We started kissing, the intensity of our emotions pouring into each touch. That night, we shared an emotional and passionate connection, our love making a testament to the bond we had forged through shared pain and unwavering support.

10

JOURNEY TO KLANSTIA

"I've packed everything you need for the transference ritual," Kristoff whispered, handing me a brown satchel. "Remember, you are the goddess of fae. You are the fated goddess. Fated queen of all and no one else can bring peace to the realms."

Kristoff's words played on repeat even as the portal opened, used not by our crystals, but by old fae magic. I'll make a note to find those historical books and educate myself on the language.

The smell of rain lingered in the air, a stale, musky taste on my tongue. I couldn't remember the last good storm in Iticha. I closed my eyes and took a deep breath, tuning into the sounds of nature. The Firefang forest felt especially alive. Then, his scent washed over me. I wondered if I'd always sense when he was near. Was that how our bond worked? As if answering my thoughts, two strong arms wrapped around my waist, and his lips nipped at my ear.

"Smells like rain, Your Grace."

"Indeed. When was the last rainstorm in Klanstia?" I asked, tilting my head to my left to give him access to the sensitive spot on my neck. Which he greedily takes advantage of.

"Hmm. Well I'd say it's been at least twenty years. I was a child."

"Are you serious?" I looked into his eyes, no humor to be found. "How have you all been able to make it through the drought?"

Blade gives me a smirk. "The Nameless Sea is a natural water source. It's clean and endless. Plus, the world stretches beyond Klanstia and Iticha, so I imagine it rains all over the ocean."

"I see."

"Plus…" He paused to take my hand in his. My knuckles secured into his palm as he moved my body into a fighter's position. Although, it's very relaxed.

"There are elemental fae that can bend water to their will." His other hand is gripped on my hip, and we begin to move as one. Seeming like a dance across the field. "Elemental fae have deeper connection with the earth. All life has water flowing through them. So, if you really need to take a drink." We stopped next to a tree trunk. Blade released me and focused on the tree, motioning with his hands. Suddenly, water bubbled up, floating from the trunk.

I couldn't believe what I was seeing. Blade held one large bubble up to my mouth. "Drink," he said. Cautiously, I pressed my lips to it and sucked. Crisp cool water flowed down my throat.

"How did you do that? I thought you were like Beaux, a fae with dragon powers," I asked, still looking at the bubbles. One by one, Blade brought them to an empty canister, letting them flow inside. He popped a cork on the top once the last one was inside.

"You only assumed I had the same powers as my dearly departed cousin." Blade looks deep into my eyes when he says, "I am not like any other fae in Klanstia, Your Grace. If I were, do you think I'd be bonded with a goddess?"

I shook my head sideways in answer, unsure of what else I could say. "We should get moving," Demetri said from afar. "We can make it to the castle before the storm hits."

We moved on foot, through the dense foliage, shadows dancing under the canopy of ancient trees. Demetri and Jen kept the side perimeter, their senses heightened, every snap of a twig or rustle of leaves a potential threat. Blade covered the rear, his eyes scanning the darkness behind us with a predator's precision, while I took the middle, feeling the weight of our mission pressing down on me.

The forest was foreign to me, every twisted root and tangled vine a potential snare. The silence was unnerving, the kind that makes your heart beat louder in your ears. Each step forward felt like venturing deeper into a labyrinth where unseen eyes watched our every move. The peacefulness of the walk was deceptive, a thin veneer masking the tension that crackled in the air.

So much has happened in the last few months; the memories are almost surreal. From a naive queen witnessing her first illegal underground fae fighting ring to this—an edge-of-your-seat stealth mission in hostile territory. The castle loomed ahead, concealed yet undeniably there, its dark silhouette a symbol of both hope and dread. I tightened my grip on my weapon, every instinct on edge, knowing the fragile peace could break at any moment.

We drew nearer, the path narrowing, the trees closing in around us. Each breath was shallow, each heartbeat a ticking clock. We were on the edge, dangerously close. The castle stood ahead, and with it, our destiny.

Now, I'm married to one and the goddess of all.

A laugh broke free, earning me curious looks from the others but I just waved them off. When we made it to the edge of the forest, Demetri guided us around the outskirts of the village so that we wouldn't be seen. Using the water flowing under the bridge, we approached the sewage drain cover that leads under the castle.

Bile rose in my throat from the foul smell that coated the air. "Is this really the only way?" I asked, covering my nose.

"Yes, Your Majesty. If you don't want to be seen," Demetri answered.

"Okay." Jen and I took hold of the bars as they are made of a mix of iron and steel, the iron being a weakness to fae, and unscrewed them. There was a question of whether I would be able to touch them, but as my hands are not currently burning, I'd say I'm okay.

We made our way down the stairs leading to the tunnel. Thankfully, there was room for sidewalks to be made on either side of the small river. "How do you know where to go, Demetri? Didn't you grow up in the Assassin's Guild?"

Demetri took the lead, sword out and ready. Jen took the rear, Blade was directly behind me and I of course took my spot behind Demetri. The entire tunnel was lit by oil lanterns. Which, I've come to realize Klanstia doesn't like to use the crystals from the caves like Iticha did. Perhaps that was a logical move since the crystals are not unlimited.

"I've made trips into Klanstia," he answered vaguely.

"Are you implying that you've had to kill fae here?" I asked.

Demetri smiled and sighed. "It's called the Assassin's Guild for a reason. If we didn't perform the task, then we would simply be another fae guild in the realm."

“You’re an assassin?” Blade’s melodic voice came from behind me.

“Yes.”

"I heard rumors about the guild growing up. Said that they were the most ruthless of all fae," Blade responded, his tone laced with caution. The sidewalk began to morph into an uphill climb. My legs started to burn after a while. I looked at my tele-watch but couldn’t remember what time it was when we started. Not that my watch was working properly; as with all our advanced technology, it didn’t work too well on this side of the border.

After another thirty or so minutes, we made it to a flight of stairs. "On the other side of the door should be the maintenance room," Demetri stated, putting his sword up and gripping a small boot dagger between his teeth while he climbed. I pulled his arm to stop him.

"You will not kill anyone that isn’t a threat to us, understood?" My eyes pierced his, and even when he nodded, I knew Demetri would never kill an innocent.

We made it to the top. A heavy sigh escaped me as I caught my breath. I hadn't been this physically sore in a while.

"Here. Drink." Blade pushed a canteen into my hand, which I took without question.

"Aren't you a goddess?" Jen asked through gulps of water.

"That's what they tell me," I responded, drinking some more and then handing it back to my mate.

"Then why are you so exhausted?" she asked.

"Good question. Once I know the answer, you will too." Jen smiled at me, and when I locked eyes with Blade again, he gave me a knowing smirk. He knew.

"We should get moving," Blade said before I had the chance to ask him what he knew. Demetri and Jen took the lead while I hung back with Blade, stopping him for a second to whisper in his ear. "Don't think you can walk away from me so easily."

"Nothing is easy with you, Your Grace." He gave me a swift kiss on the lips before following the others.

As we made it through the service entrance, the eerie silence of the castle greeted us. It was mid-day, yet there was no one around. No servants bustling about, no guards patrolling. The absence of any staff was unsettling, a clear indication that something was off. Shouldn't there be at least a maid cleaning? Out past the service entrance, through their quarters, we entered a narrow hallway. To the right would lead us towards the throne hall and all the sleeping quarters. If we went left, the training yards and the armory.

"Where would the crown be kept?" I asked no one in particular.

"I imagine if it isn't in the throne room, then it would be in the vault," Blade answered. "I think we should split up. You two survey the castle."

“What if we run in to anyone?” Jen asked.

Blade looked around then back at her. “There is no one in the castle except for us.”

“How can you be so sure?” Demetri spoke this time.

“Because we would have seen a worker by now. Maybe even a guard,” Blade responded then looked to me. “We will go get the crown.”

I followed Blade down the left hallway towards the throne hall and sleeping quarters on the main level. From what I gathered the last time I was in this place, there are three levels. We walked in silence, nothing but the heels of our boots tapping along the paved path of the hall-stone floor. When suddenly, I pulled into a dark room. A hand wrapped around my mouth, a thick arm holding me in a warm embrace.

"We're not alone as I suspected, Your Grace." Blade's warm words kissed against my ear. "I need you to remain still." I nodded.

A few heartbeats passed before I was spun around to face him. His lips crashing to mine, a hand gripping both wrists above my head. It was unexpected but I didn't fight him. His free hand went to my waist as our tongues clashed together. Blade let go of my wrist so he could grip my breast, the fabric of my shirt sensitive against my pebbling nipples.

Our kiss didn't break as he lifted me from the floor. I wrapped my legs around him, running my fingers through his black curls until my back landed on something soft. A bed. Is he going to fuck me in someone else's room?

Blade's lips left mine, moving to my chin, my neck, then clamping around my breast through my shirt. His hands tugged it above my head until I was bare before him. Next, my boots and pants followed.

He moved down my body, peppering my hot skin with his kisses until landing on the apex of my thighs.

"Fuck," I moaned at his first lick. Mouth sucking my clit while two fingers pumped in and out of me. My hands found his hair, I gripped, pushing his face into my pussy. His tongue moved in sync with his fingers. His other hand played with the peak of my breast. I bucked my hips with each movement, matching his pace until I took control. Riding out my orgasm on his tongue.

When his crimson eyes met mine again, I saw myself coating his lips. His clothes were gone in the next second. Then he crawled on top of me, but before he plunged inside of me, I flipped us. "You need to relax, husband," I whispered into his ear before nipping at his neck, sucking hard enough to leave my mark. I gripped his thick shaft, lining the head of his cock with my entrance before sinking down onto him. We groaned in bliss. I waited to allow my body to adjust to his size. Being that I was a virgin up until a few nights ago, I still was not used to him.

My nails pressed into his chest, feeling the smooth curves of his muscles shift with my touch. I rocked my hips, while one of his hands found my clit and the other settled on my hip. We moved in perfect sync, just like that first night. My soul stretched out, yearning to connect with his. When our eyes locked once more, I knew I would be with him forever.

11

ONE MORE NIGHT

"So, this is your room?" I asked, our bodies still warm from ecstasy.

He looked at me and smiled, brushing a strand from my eyes before answering. "How did you guess?"

"Well," I looked around the room, noting how simple it was, "first, I do not believe you would fuck me in another man's bed."

"That's where you're wrong, Your Grace." His crimson eyes narrow with intensity. "I would have you anyway and anywhere I could. If you let me." I felt heat rise to my cheeks at the declarations. "Especially when you call me husband."

I couldn't stop the smile that broke free. It's a feeling I never want to go away. "I thought we were going to look for the crown?"

Blade sighed as if he dreaded the thought of finding it. "I just wanted us to have one more night of peace before you face-off against my cousin. I imagine once you adorn it, then you will call her to challenge."

"Of course, our realm needs peace not continued war. Do you not agree with my decision?"

"If it were up to me, I'd send your best assassin to slit her throat."

"But it isn't up to you."

Blade smiled again, those dimples appearing before we both moved to sit up against the headboard. "I like your room."

"Really?" I nodded my head up and down. "It isn't too simple for your liking?"

I chuckled. "Clearly you do not know your wife too well. A bedroom," I started before climbing to straddle him. I could feel him starting to get hard again. Purposefully, I rolled my hips, encouraging him. I leaned forward, caressing his lips with mine, as I continued to tease him.

"What are bedrooms meant for, Your Grace?" he whispered against my lips.

"Hmm," I leaned to answer him in his ear, "fucking and sleeping."

A growl rumbled in his throat, my pussy clenched missing the feel of him inside of me. "Oh, and do you want to sleep, Your Grace?"

I answered him without words. Kissing him deeply, rubbing my wet pussy up and down his erection. My clit buzzed with the friction and I could feel myself chasing an orgasm. "One more night of making love to you, Blade. I'll sleep when I'm dead."

Blade gripped my hips hard, helping to bring my orgasm forward, but he didn't let me recover as he flipped us plunging himself deep inside of me. We spent the next several hours naked in each other's arms. Taking breaks to eat and use the bathroom. And when Demetri and Jen came to find us to report that we were in fact the only four beings in the entire palace and that they had secured the fae crown, I didn't want to face the decision tonight. When the sun finally set, I found myself falling in blissful sleep in the arms of my husband. Something I never thought I would ever get the chance to do.

Tomorrow would be a new day. The day that I would restore peace to the realm of Klanstia and Iticha. It would also be the day that I choose to erase my humanity from me. Tonight would be etched in my memory. The feelings of pure happiness couldn't possibly be erased, could it?

12

THE FAE CROWN

Morning came and with it, the decision I did not want to have to make. With the fae ring on my left finger, I gripped the fae crown in my palms. Magic, buzzed in my hands as my essence recognized the power of my ethereal mother. Kristoff's warning played on repeat in my head. I scanned the three faces that were waiting for my next move. Did they understand the gravity of the situation? Should I tell them what I will lose? What I intend to give up? Or does it matter if it means saving them all?

If I fail, I could lose everything. My sister, my home, my husband. Jen and Demetri, the remaining soldiers, and every citizen that is loyal to me would become slaves.

I stood in the center of the throne hall, where I first met Tomas Feynard; a place where I bartered for peace and promised to marry the late fae king to prevent war. My gaze shifted to the far balcony doors, and the pain of the memory with Beaux there threatened to overwhelm me. Without hesitation, I walked toward them, savoring the cool air against my skin as the sunlight embraced me. With the crown in my left hand, I approached the edge, running my right hand along the smooth stone ledge. I heard footsteps behind me but knew it was Blade, so I stayed still. His scent warmed me, and the spark inside me reached for him. My twin flame. "The last time I was standing on this balcony, I was just a human who thought she was doing what was best for her people."

"You're still her, regardless of the decision you make," he says, stepping up to my right. "Just take what you have learned and let it help you with this choice."

"But what if I choose wrong again? What if I do what I'm destined to do but it backfires, and our entire world is destroyed? What if—" My words are cut off with a hard kiss on my lips.

Blade steps backwards, my chin capture between his index finger and thumb. Those crimson eyes I've gotten so lost in, pierce into me as he reminds me, "You must stop living your life by 'what if' scenarios. You are Peech Whittington, daughter of the Goddess Lasir. Granddaughter of the God Naxian, Goddess of all Fae, and the keeper of my heart."

I smiled at the last admission. "I have to make a terrible choice." My words are whispered between the two of us.

"Whatever you choose, you will have me."

"But you don't even know—"

"I know that I'm in love with you." Gods, his gaze was so intense, the truth of his words had me melting in his arms.

"You can't. We've only known each other for almost two weeks."

"I know."

"But how?"

"Because I knew the moment I set my eyes on you that I was irrevocably in love with you. I saw you standing in the crowd. Your eyes filled with so much rage over the injustice that was being done to five fae. I told myself that I would marry you. No matter what I needed to do, I would win your heart over." I swallowed as he continued. "You have completed me, Peech Whittington. I was a lost soul until you found mine. There is nothing that would ever keep me from loving you."

What could I say to that? Did I love him the way he loves me? "Blade, I—"

"It's okay that you don't feel the same. Right now, if all you feel for me is lust, then I'm happy to wait."

"I do not know how long it will take me to fall in love again, Blade. Beaux, he was my first and only love."

"Here's the beautiful thing about being the twin flame to a goddess." He leaned forward, his nose brushing against mine as our foreheads pressed together. "You will find me in this life and the next. One day, when you grow to love me as I do, you will come looking for me. It doesn't matter where my body maybe, my soul will always guide yours to it. So you see, I will wait for eternity."

"Blade, eternity is such a long time. You will waste your mortal life waiting. Especially after I sacrifice my humanity for the sake of peace." Shit. I bit my tongue the moment the words slipped from my mouth.

Blade lifted his head to meet my gaze. "What do you mean, sacrifice your humanity?"

"I mean, tear the human parts of me away. Leaving nothing but the goddess." Blade stepped away from me. His large hand was rubbing the fine hairs along his chin as if he were trying to put a puzzle together. "Blade, that's why I haven't adorned the crown yet. I must perform a ritual before putting it on. Once I finish the spell, I'll be freed from my human self."

Blade's back was to me. His arms were slack at his side, while his hands were balled into fists. I saw the tension in his shoulders as the muscles in his neck twitched. He was angry.

"This is why you can't be in love with me. Regardless of us being married, it will only be in name from this day forward. There will be no future home. No children sharing our blood. When I take my final place as goddess of fae, you will be a widower. You'll be free to wed again."

Blade spun on his heels, charging at me with haste and rage. My back hit the wall as I was momentarily surprised by his reaction. His palms landed on my hips in a bruising grip, lips crashing against mine until I relented, allowing him access. Our tongues clashed, and the fae crown fell from my grip. The skirts of my dress were pushed up against my hip, my undergarment torn, before I heard his pants being pulled down. Blade pushed his cock deep inside my pussy in one thrust.

He deepened the kiss as he lifted me from the ground. I wrapped my legs around him. His thrust were hard. Blade was claiming me. Marking my body with his mouth. And I let him. It was quick and when he came inside of me, we stayed against the wall until he caught his breath. Those two crimson eyes pierced my soul, holding my attention.

"You are mine, Peech Whittington." He went to his shirt, pulling it sideways to reveal our mate mark. "And I am yours. There will be no other for me. I will be at your side for all eternity. I'm your husband and you are my wife. Regardless of who or what you are. In case you forget, look at the symbol emblazoned over your heart."

His lips met mine again but this time it was softer. I rested my forehead against his as we inhaled each other's scent. Even without my humanity, at least I knew I would always have him. "We should head inside and prepare for the ritual," I said.

But Blade didn't move. He looked at me before pulling out, then did something unexpected. "What are you doing?" I looked around as he crawled underneath the skirts of my dress.

"You didn't come. What kind of husband would I be if I didn't let you enjoy the pleasure of my tongue?" Heat rose to my cheeks at that, but I knew I had nothing to fear. And when he licked me, sucking my clit, it was pure bliss.

After we cleaned up in a nearby bathroom, we went back to the throne hall where Jen and Demetri were waiting. We stopped before opening the throne hall door as we both heard noises coming from inside.

"Will she be mad if she catches us?" Demetri asked. Blade moved to the small opening between the doors then waved me over.

"Looks like we weren't the only ones biding our time with sex." Blade whispered as I looked inside. Jen had Demetri on his back, their clothes and weapons completely discarded. She was in charge, as I suspected any of my generals would be when it came to the bedroom.

"Well, I'll be damned. When do you think that started?" I asked before turning to give them their privacy.

"I think it started back before you found us, but this is their first time having sex," he answered so confidently.

"And how do you know that?"

"Because I overheard them in the hot springs one night at Kristoff's." Blade's lips caressed my ear as he whispered, "You're not the only one who enjoyed being mouth fucked in those illustrious springs."

I could feel the heat rising in my cheeks as I clenched my pussy with the memory. Our first time being intimate with one another. "How long do you think we have?" I asked.

"I'd say we should get them when the ceremony is over," Blade suggested.

"You think it will be wise for us to do it alone?"

"I don't think it matters who is with you, Your Grace."

I nodded and we headed back to Blade's chambers to gather the items Kristoff gave me for the ritual. "There is a clearing in the back we could use," Blade said as he gathered his own previsions, for what, I'm not sure.

"Why are you packing?"

Blade turned to me before responding. "Because we need to leave as soon as you're powered up."

Right. "Okay. Make sure you pack for me too."

"Of course." After we left his room, I followed Blade through the castle until we were about to walk out to the training yard. "What's wrong?"

Blade's ears were twitching, nose sniffing the air and I could sense he was on high alert. "Nothing, I just thought I heard someone."

"You think we're not alone?" I scanned the area, using my sense to detect anyone else but no one was coming up on my radar except for Blade, Jen, Demetri, and— "No!"

Blade's body was jerked backwards. The sound of his bones crunching against the wall as the large spear pierced through his body armor directly into his heart.

“Run.” He coughed trying to wave me off of him as I attempted to help him up.

More spears came whizzing by. Each clattering to the floor or splintering at the hard contact made with the stone wall.

“Blade, you have to get up.” I encourage, trying to keep myself from shedding tears. “I will not lose you.”

“Go.” He coughed, blood splattered across my face. I drowned out all other noise to tune in to his heart. It was beating too quickly. If I didn't do something to save him, Blade would die.

A roar of an army came floading in from the walls beyond the yard. Fae dressed in armor came charging at us. In the lead, Princess Plum. Her violet armor shimmered in the light as she marched toward us. I stood between them and Blade. Reaching for my weapons only to realize I didn’t have them on me. How could I be so foolish to think we were safe here?

The army stopped a few feet from us. Plum came up to me but stopped just two feet away. A dagger could pierce straight through her eyeball at this distance.

"Queen Peech Whittington, I expected more from the goddess who killed my father and brothers." Her voice was coated in hate. Each word seemed to slide over me like a snake does a vine.

"I need to heal him, or he will die," I stated. Her purple gaze went past me to where Blade lay. He passed out, but I could hear his heart still beat which gave me some hope.

"Why haven't you already healed him?" she questioned. "Aren't you supposed to be this all powerful being?" Plum laughed. Her attempt at insulting me not working because I didn't care about myself.

"Do what you want with me, but until Blade is healed, your gloating tactics will not work."

Plum smiled at the challenge. "I'm not trying to fight you, goddess. All I want is to be rid of you so that your people can finally accept me as their queen."

I shook my head. "My people do not want a dictator, Plum."

She snarled. "I'll fight you for the crown."

I raised a brow in question. "I don't have time for this. Blade is dying."

"Why do you care what happens to my cousin?" Her scrutinizing gaze traveled between us, then, when it landed on my wedding band, she laughed. A deep belly laugh for a few heartbeats.

I just need to keep her distracted so Demetri and Jen can get to a better vantage point. My mind is distracted as I try to stay in-tune with Blade's fading life and Plum's annoyingly long monologue. "You let me heal him and I will fight you for the crown."

That shut her up.

"To the death," she responded.

"Fine." I slowly backed away until I could kneel next to Blade, but also not turn my back towards the fae army and my challenger. I placed a hand on his head and the other where the spear was piercing through. A moment later, Jen and Demetri came running up to my side, the fae army went to attack, but Plum stopped them.

"I have challenged the queen. That means no one is to attack her soldiers until the victor is claimed." The soldiers all stood erect at her command.

"I'm so sorry." Jen was on the verge of tears.

"None of that matters. I'm going to have to heal him, but I need you two to take him away from here. Portal to the Crystal Caves where Maya is. She'll be able to help him with the rest." Jen and Demetri looked weary as they watched the blood slowly spill from the sides of the spear that entered his stomach. “We can’t leave you,” Demetri whispered.

“You don’t have a choice.” I started to get control of my breathing, unsure how I knew what to do but something inside of me, the fae parts, told me what to do. My eyes closed and it was as if an instruction manual opened up to me. My essence poured into him. “Peech!” Jen’s voice was panicked. “Your Majesty!” Demetri yelled. They sounded frightened but was it of me? Or did Plum attack them? “You’ve given me enough, wife.” This time, Blade’s voice cut through. Only he was calm. I searched for him but all I felt was his soul. “Go back. If you give me anymore, you won’t have the strength to fight her.” “But I can’t lose you.” My voice croaked on un-shed tears.“You won’t.”

13

THE REALM IS WON

I opened my eyes, to find that Jen, Demetri, and Blade were gone. Only the small pool of Blade's blood remained. A slight pink glow illuminated from my hands and when I turned to face the princess, she appeared to be stunned in place. Her mouth was agape, and I could have sworn I could sense fear in her.

"What…where did they go? Did you do something to them?" I charged toward her but a shield of magic went up around her.

"I didn't do anything. You sent them away, goddess," Plum replied. Her tone weary.

"But I can't teleport people."

"I get the feeling you don't know what you can do with the gifts you were given." Plum lowered her shield then sighed. The stoic mask back in place. "No matter, we still have to fight. And I'd like to add one more rule if you're okay with it?" I arched my brow. "No magic. It must be hand to hand or weapon to weapon."

"Fair enough." Now that, I can do.

"Then follow me."

I trailed the princess out to what I suspect was the clearing that Blade was attempting to bring me to. It seemed like it was built for the purpose of fighting with the circle ranging from twenty feet wide. Worn dirt from years of training was well compacted in the spot.

"First, we need the fae crown and ring placed on the pedestal," Princess Plum demanded. I looked down at the fae ring, pulled it off and walked towards the mantle. "And now the crown."

"I'm not sure where it is," I answered honestly, placing the ring at the center. In the next second, I felt magic come around it. A sheen of transparent color glinted in the sun.

“The magic shield that will only break once the victor is claimed. Now, the fae crown must be around here somewhere. General Josalen!” she singsonged.

“You know she isn’t here,” I snapped.

“Are you sure about that?”

“Deadly.”

Plum shrugged her shoulders but out of the corner of my eye, I saw her and my heart dropped. My body whirled to face her, but as I saw the chains around her neck, connecting to her wrist and binding to her ankles, relief flooded me.

“Oh, oh, you thought she betrayed you?” Plum’s dark laughter fueled my rage. “Nope, I snagged her just before she blipped away with the other two.” Jen put the fae crown over the ring and the magic shield closed around them.

“Let her go,” I snarled.

“No, little Miss General will be here to make sure you play by the rules.” Plum narrowed her eyes at me. “My rules.”

“I have honor, Plum. Do you?”

“Honor doesn’t win realms. Fear does,” she retorted.

Princess Plum has no idea what it takes to be a ruler. To even be a leader. I shook my head in disappointment at her. "Let's get this over with."

We went to our respective sides of the ring. There would be no signal to start us, but I knew from my training that fighting hand to hand, I needed to learn my opponent. Let her come to me.

The arena was silent, the air thick with anticipation as I faced Princess Plum. Our eyes locked, each of us knowing that only one would leave alive. The crowd held its breath as we circled each other, our movements fluid and precise.

I made the first move, lunging with my fist aimed at her jaw. She dodged, countering with a swift kick that I barely blocked. The clash of our bodies echoed through the arena, each strike met with equal force. We were evenly matched, our skills and strength a mirror of each other.

Sweat dripped down my brow as I parried a series of rapid punches from Plum. I retaliated with a powerful roundhouse kick, but she ducked and swept my legs out from under me. I hit the ground hard, but rolled to my feet in an instant, my eyes blazing with determination.

The fight raged on, neither of us gaining a clear advantage. Then, in a desperate move, Plum scooped up a handful of dirt and flung it into my face. I staggered back, blinded, and she seized the opportunity. She tackled me to the ground, her hands closing around my throat.

I gasped for air, my vision blurring as her grip tightened. The world seemed to slow, the sounds of the crowd fading into the background. Summoning the last of my strength, I twisted my body, using my legs to push her off balance. With a final, powerful shove, I knocked her to the ground.

Gasping for breath, I stood over my fallen enemy. I could end it now, but something in her eyes gave me pause. Instead of delivering the final blow, I extended a hand, offering mercy.

I turned to claim the fae crown and ring from the victor's circle, but Plum, driven by rage and humiliation, lunged at me from behind. Before she could reach me, General Jen Josalen intercepted the attack. With a swift, practiced motion, Jen wrapped her chains around Plum, the sound of bones snapping echoing through the arena as Plum's neck broke.

I stood tall, the crown and ring now mine. The fae army standing erect, I could sense the unease from some of them. Should they attack me for their princess being dead? No, they won't.

"Fae army, I stand before you as a victor. You will now obey the commands of my General. Jen Josalen of Eastend." The Fae all stood at attention, a salute of submission rippling through them as their right fist went over their armored hearts. I turned to face Jen, breaking the chains from her body. "I need to perform the ritual now."

"What ritual?" she asked.

"Just trust me."

"Always."

I walked over to where my bag lay discarded on the ground, my heart still pounding from the fight. I needed the items for the ritual to take over the fae crown and ring. But when I opened the bag, there was nothing inside except a rolled-up parchment. Confused, I unrolled it and found a letter from Kristoff.

"You only needed to believe you could win to bring peace to the realm. Here is a list of instructions from your grandfather Naxian."

I read the letter in silence, absorbing the words. My grandfather's wisdom had always guided me, and now it seemed he had one final lesson to impart. I folded the parchment carefully and went back to General Jen Josalen.

"We need to get back to the Crystal Caves," I told her. "Maya and the rest of our family are waiting for us."

I called upon a general in the fae army, Zain. "General Zain, take control over Klansita until I can give you further instructions."

Jen offered to stay behind, which I didn't agree with at first. But then I relented. Jen was the only person in Klansita I could trust. "Alright, Jen. Stay and keep things in order. I'll be back soon."

Finally, I figured out how to use my wings. Calling them forward, I transformed into my goddess form and flew to the Crystal Caves. As I landed, Maya, my bonded dragon, greeted me warmly.

"Thank you for caring for my younger sister, Patrice," I said, hugging her.

There was a heartfelt reunion with young Patrice, who was eleven, and Demetri. To my surprise, General Sierra Scarr, my Westend General who I thought was killed, was also there. Sierra revealed that Maya had saved her.

I looked around and saw my mate and husband, Blade, resting. I decided to reunite with him later in private. Gathering my friends, I laid out the plan.

“General Sierra Scarr and I will travel to Iticha to restore it to peace. Demetri, you will go to Klansita to be with General Jen Josalen. Patrice, you will stay with Maya until I summon you. Blade will remain here in the healing part of the Crystal Caves.”

I stood at the edge of the border, the night sky stretching endlessly above us, dotted with stars that seemed to whisper ancient secrets. Maya, my bonded dragon, stood beside me, her scales shimmering in the moonlight. The weight of the fae crown and ring felt heavy in my hands, a tangible reminder of the power and responsibility they carried.

Maya's eyes, wise and knowing, locked onto mine. Her presence was a comfort, a steadying force amidst the chaos of my thoughts.

"I will return them to their rightful place," I told her, my voice firm but tinged with uncertainty. "It’s about time I meet my mother."

Maya's deep, rumbling voice filled my mind. Are you sure about this, Peech? The path ahead is fraught with danger and unknowns.

I nodded, though my heart pounded with a mixture of fear and determination. "I have to, Maya. For too long, I've run from my past, from my true heritage. It's time to face it head-on, to embrace who I am meant to be."

Maya's gaze softened, and she lowered her massive head until it was level with mine. You have grown so much, my rider. You are stronger than you realize. But remember, the power of the crown and ring is seductive. It can corrupt even the purest of hearts. I tightened my grip on the artifacts, feeling their energy pulse through me. "I will not let it consume me. I'll use their power for the greater good, to bring peace and unity to our lands." Maya nodded slowly, her eyes reflecting a mixture of pride and concern. Then we shall face this journey together. Whatever comes, we will stand as one. I reached out, resting my hand on Maya's snout, feeling the warmth and strength of her bond. "Thank you, Maya. Your support means everything to me. For keeping my sister safe and protecting our borders." With a final glance at the night sky, I turned towards the path that would lead me to my mother, the fae queen. The journey would be perilous, but with Maya by my side and a heart resolute in purpose, I felt ready to confront whatever lay ahead.

Conclusion

Queen Peech and her husband Blade traveled throughout Klanstia and Iticha, their presence a beacon of hope and strength. Together, they brought peace and prosperity to both realms, their love and unity inspiring all who witnessed their journey. The Council of Generals ruled wisely, their decisions guided by the wisdom and fairness of Queen Peech, who had the final say on laws and diplomatic matters.

Years passed, and under their leadership, the realms flourished. The once war-torn lands now thrived with vibrant communities, bustling markets, and flourishing arts. Peech's heart swelled with pride and contentment as she saw the fruits of their labor. When Queen Peech's sister Patrice came of age, it was time for a new chapter. Patrice had grown into a wise and compassionate leader, her character molded by the lessons and wisdom Peech had imparted. Peech saw in her sister the same strength and resolve that had driven her own journey.

Peech and Blade decided to retire to the realm of gods, where they would live for eternity. But before they left, Peech had one final task. She visited the realm of gods, the fae crown and ring in hand. Her mother, Lasir, was there, but she didn't even remember her own daughter. At first, Peech thought she would be hurt by this, but then she realized that time wasted on anyone who would willingly abandon their family wasn't worth it. As she returned the fae crown and ring to their rightful place, she felt a sense of closure and inner peace wash over her. It was a profound moment of acceptance and release, coming to terms with the end of her active role in the world of mortals.

Back in the mortal realms, Patrice took up the mantle of leadership, guided by the teachings and legacy of her sister. Under her stewardship, the Council of Generals continued to rule with wisdom and justice, ensuring that the peace Peech and Blade had fought so hard to achieve would endure. Patrice's reign was marked by her own innovations and deep empathy, qualities that endeared her to her people and strengthened the bonds within the realm.

In the realm of gods, Peech and Blade found a new kind of peace. They watched over the realms from afar, their love and legacy living on in the hearts of those they had touched. They knew that their journey had been worth every struggle, every sacrifice. Peech often reflected on the tranquility she felt, her spirit at ease with the knowledge that she had fulfilled her destiny and left a lasting legacy.The impact of Peech and Blade's reign was felt for generations. Their policies and reforms continued to shape the governance of Klanstia and Iticha, fostering a culture of fairness, innovation, and unity.

Their love story became a legend, a testament to the power of courage and the unyielding spirit of true leaders. The realms of Klanstia and Iticha thrived, forever grateful to the queen who had believed in herself and brought peace to their lands. And so, Queen Peech and Blade lived for eternity, their story a timeless reminder of the transformative power of love, bravery, and wisdom. The realms prospered under the shadow of their legacy, always looking to the future with hope and determination.

ABOUT THE AUTHOR

C.M. Hano is a small-town author currently living just thirty minutes from NOLA. Her love for Adult Fantasy inspires her to continue to create magical worlds readers can escape to. She is best known for her Romantasy title: “Once And Future Queen,” and various other fantasy romance. She lives a charming life with her husband and two daughters.

STAY IN TOUCH

Facebook: C. M. Hano
Twitter: @HanoCera
Instagram: @cerahano
TikTok: @cmhano_author
Facebook Reading Group: C. M. Hano’s Bookdragons
Website: cmhanoauthor.com

www.ingramcontent.com/pod-product-compliance
Lightning Source LLC
LaVergne TN
LVHW010608110826
845149LV00003B/816

* 9 7 9 8 9 9 5 4 6 7 1 7 5 *